Nancy Drew®
in
The Clue of the Dancing Puppet

Nancy Drew Mystery Stories® in Armada

* For contractual reasons, Armada has been obliged to publish from No. 51 onwards before publishing Nos. 47–50. These missing numbers will be published as soon as possible.

Nancy Drew Mystery Stories®

The Clue of the Dancing Puppet

Carolyn Keene

ARMADA

First published in the U.K. in 1972 by
William Collins Sons & Co. Ltd, London and Glasgow
First published in Armada in 1978
This impression 1990

Armada is an imprint of
the Children's Division, part of
the Collins Publishing Group,
8 Grafton Street, London W1X 3LA

Printed and bound in Great Britain by
William Collins Sons & Co. Ltd, Glasgow

CONTENTS

The Mysterious Dancer

"I WONDER why Dad sent for me," Nancy said to Mr Drew's pleasant secretary, as she waited in the outer room of her father's office.

Miss Johnson smiled. "I would guess it's some kind of a mystery your father wants you to solve. He'll soon be finished with the client he has in there. Tell me, how are Bess and George?"

Nancy, titian blonde and attractive, chuckled. "At the moment Bess is—well, stage-struck. She has been slimming in order to get a part in one of the Footlighters' plays."

"Oh, the amateur group," said Miss Johnson.

"Yes. Bess belongs to it and has been trying to interest George and me," Nancy replied. "But I thought it might tie me down too much if a mystery came along for me to work on. And George has been busy playing in a series of tennis tournaments."

George Fayne, a bright-eyed, athletic girl, and pretty Bess Marvin were cousins. They often found themselves involved in mysteries with Nancy Drew, who was their closest friend.

At this moment Miss Johnson's desk phone buzzed.

She picked it up. "Yes, Mr Drew." The secretary turned to Nancy. "Your father wants you to come in and meet his client. He's an actor," she added.

"An actor!" Nancy echoed, intrigued. She rose and entered her father's office.

Mr Drew kissed his daughter, then he said, "Nancy, I'd like to present Mr Hamilton Spencer."

Nancy shook hands with the tall, slender man. She guessed from his greying hair that he was about sixty years of age. His voice was deep and resonant, and he had a winning smile.

"Mr Spencer is a professional actor, Nancy," Mr Drew went on. "He and his wife have been engaged by the Footlighters to coach their plays. I met Mr and Mrs Spencer when I was asked to draw up their contract."

Nancy listened attentively, but she was sure this information was not the reason her father had asked her to come to his office.

To Mr Spencer, she said, "My friend Bess Marvin tells me the old Van Pelt estate, which was given to the Footlighters, is ideal for your performances."

"Yes, it is," Mr Spencer replied. "The first floor of the house is given over to offices and dressing-rooms. Mrs Spencer and I and a friend live on the second floor. The large hay barn is our theatre."

As he paused, looking at Mr Drew, the lawyer smiled. "Please tell Nancy your story. Since she's an amateur detective, I think this mystery would intrigue her."

Mr Spencer reddened a bit, and Nancy sensed he was embarrassed to think that a girl of eighteen might solve a mystery which was baffling a man of his years and experience.

"For several months after we moved to the Footlighters' new home," he began, "everything was peaceful. Then recently a strange occurrence has been repeated several times. I must confess it has my wife and me jittery. At night a life-size puppet in ballet costume has been seen dancing in various places—on the lawn, on the deserted stage, even on the flat roof of a shed."

"It sounds fantastic," Nancy remarked. "Are you sure this isn't a real person?"

"Indeed I am," Mr Spencer answered. "I've been an actor for enough years to differentiate between live actors and artificial ones. I don't know how she is operated, but this dancer is a puppet all right—of the marionette type. What I want to know is, *where* does she come from and *why*!"

"Have you ever followed the puppet?" Nancy asked Mr Spencer.

"Oh, yes, twice. But before I could get near her, she disappeared. That ghostly dancer is getting me down. I can't sleep. Something *has* to be done!"

Mr Drew interrupted the actor, who was showing signs of becoming unnerved by his own recital. "Nancy, the Spencers feel that there must be something behind this strange performance—perhaps even some sinister plot against the Footlighters."

Mr Spencer nodded vigorously. "Common sense tells me there *must* be. Nancy, would you be willing to come out to the estate and stay with us for a while? From what your father has told me, you might be able to bring about an end to this strange drama."

Nancy turned to her father. "You know I'd love to go," she said. "Is it all right with you, Dad?"

Mr Drew smiled. "I'll give my consent on one condition—that Bess and George go with you. George Fayne, a girl, is Bess Marvin's cousin," he explained to Mr Spencer.

"My wife Margo and I would be very happy to have all three girls as our guests," Mr Spencer said quickly. He rose to leave. "Nancy, will you ask your friends and phone me their answer this evening? And please don't disappoint me."

As the actor put his hand on the doorknob, he said, "This whole thing must be kept very confidential." He snapped the fingers of his free hand. "I have it! Nancy and George must join the Footlighters. Then no one will question their reason for being around the estate."

Mr Spencer had barely left when Miss Johnson announced that another client was waiting.

"I'll see him in a minute," Mr Drew told her. Then he turned to Nancy. "Just one word of advice, young lady. *Be careful!* You know you're the only detective I have!"

Nancy laughed, kissed her father, and said, "See you at supper?"

"Yes. And I'll be starved. Tell Hannah to prepare one of her super-duper dinners." Hannah Gruen was the pleasant, faithful housekeeper who had managed the Drew household and helped to bring up Nancy since she was three. At that time Mrs Drew had died from a sudden illness.

As soon as Nancy reached home she phoned Bess and George, inviting them to supper and suggesting they come early, as she had something important to tell them. When they accepted, Nancy and Mrs Gruen discussed the menu.

"Let's cook the roast that's in the refrigerator," Nancy suggested. "And have strawberry shortcake for dessert with all the trimmings. Oh, I forgot. Bess is dieting. We'd better change that to apple snow pudding with thin custard sauce."

Nancy offered to set the table and had just finished when the bell rang. Bess and George arrived together. George literally dragged Nancy into the living-room.

"Out with it! Something important's brewing!" she exclaimed.

Nancy laughed, then told the story of the mysterious dancing puppet. George frowned, puzzled. Bess drew in a deep breath. She gave a mock shiver, then burst out:

"How divine! Imagine living in the same house with a real actor and actress!"

"And a supernatural one," George reminded her cousin.

"But Nancy didn't say the dancing puppet came into the house," Bess argued.

"The puppet may enter any time. She's already been in the theatre," George teased.

Nancy interrupted to ask, "Can you girls come with me? I promised to let Mr Spencer know tonight."

"Of course."

"You bet."

At once, Nancy called the actor, who was delighted. "We'll expect you tomorrow afternoon," he told her.

"Margo and I have a late breakfast at one. We're late sleepers due to the night shows."

When Nancy returned, she told George about the plan to have them join the Footlighters.

"Wonderful!" Bess exclaimed. "You'll love it. And, Nancy, you'll get a part right away. You often had the lead in the school plays."

"No, thanks. I'm going to the estate to do some detective work. I'll sign up to help paint scenery."

George grinned. "I couldn't recite a nursery rhyme. Put me down for odd jobs like scene shifting—my muscles are hard!"

Bess went to the phone and called Janet Wood, the secretary of the Footlighters' membership committee. "There's to be a meeting tonight," said Janet, who was a good friend of Bess's. "I'll bring the application forms to Nancy's house and wait while they fill them in. Then I'll hand the cards over to the committee tonight to be voted on. But Nancy and George will get in. Don't worry."

Janet Wood arrived in half an hour. Nancy and George filled in the cards, and Bess and Janet acted as sponsors. "I'm thrilled that you're joining," said Janet, as she was leaving. "I'll call you tonight after the meeting."

True to her promise, Janet phoned Bess at Nancy's house soon after ten. The one-sided conversation lasted a long while. Finally Bess returned to the living-room.

"You'll get formal notices in the mail," she said without enthusiasm. "But you're in."

George snorted. "You seem about as happy over it as an actress who didn't pass her screen test."

"I'm puzzled," Bess admitted. "Since you're new members, perhaps I shouldn't tell you. But because you're also detectives, I will."

Bess revealed that the membership committee, including the president and Janet, consisted of seven men and women. One of them, Tammi Whitlock, had spoken very forcefully against admitting Nancy and George.

"You don't know Tammi. She's rather new here in River Heights," Bess explained. "Been here about six months. Tammi came from California and is living in town with an aunt. She's our leading lady at the moment, and I must say she's an excellent actress."

"But why would she vote against *us*?" George queried. "I could see that she might not want any competition in the acting line, and she *may* have heard about Nancy's ability from the others. But of course Nancy didn't sign up for that. So why the big objection from Tammi?"

Nancy had no comment other than to say she was eager to meet Tammi Whitlock and find out the reason for her objections, if possible.

"There's a performance tomorrow night," Bess said. "We have only four a week. You can meet Tammi after the show. Well, let's go home, George. Shall we be ready to start about three o'clock tomorrow, Nancy? And will you pick us up in your convertible?"

"Sure thing," Nancy promised, as she saw her friends to the door.

Promptly at three o'clock the next day, Nancy picked up the girls, and Bess directed her along one of the tree-shaded roads on the outskirts of River Heights. Several old houses, set well back from the road, could be glimpsed through the heavy growth of trees and shrubbery.

"Next driveway on your left," Bess said presently.

At the entrance an artistic wooden plaque hanging from a tree announced:

THE FOOTLIGHTERS

The long, tree-lined driveway curved to the right, then to the left. Ahead, beyond a wide lawn, stood a large white, three-storey house of the early nineteen hundred period. The windows on the main floor were long, narrow and shuttered. On the second floor, there were many bays and dormers, each with a carved arch above.

Nancy parked near the front porch which extended across the front of the house, and the girls carried their bags into the wide centre hall. Mr Spencer, smiling broadly, came down the stairs and was introduced to George.

"Mighty glad you're here," he said in welcome. "My wife is out, and I have to run over to the theatre immediately. But I'll show you to your rooms first."

He took Nancy's bag, telling the other girls he would come back for theirs. The steep stairway led to a long hallway on the second floor, with bedrooms on each side and a rear stairway down to the kitchen.

"Margo and I have the front room," Mr Spencer said. "You girls will have this one, which also faces the front, and the one opposite, which overlooks the gardens at the back. This door"— he pointed to a third door in the centre of the hall—"hides a stairway to the attic. I've never been up there"— his eyes twinkled— "but, Nancy, I'm sure that's one place you'll want to investigate."

"There's one more door—at the end of the hall near the kitchen stairway," George remarked. "Is that where your friend sleeps?"

"Yes. Emmet Calhoun is over at the theatre just now. Well, make yourselves at home, girls. See you later." He left them.

Nancy chose the rear bedroom, which gave her a good view of the playhouse. It was a large red barn with a smaller wing. To one side of the building was a wide parking area.

The girls began to unpack their belongings. In a few minutes Nancy was settled. "I'm going to follow Mr Spencer's hint and take a peek at the attic," she said to the others. She walked to the door, opened it, and went up the steps.

In the cousins' room, Bess giggled. "Nancy just can't wait to get started on her mystery. I'd like to have a little fun first."

"Like doing what—playing hide-and-seek in the hay-loft?" George scoffed.

At this moment the girls heard a loud thump in the attic. It was followed immediately by a second one. Bess and George ran to the attic stairway.

"Nancy! Are you all right?" they called anxiously. There was no answer.

·2·

A Startling Call

"SOMETHING has happened to Nancy!" Bess exclaimed
fearfully.

George was already racing up the attic stairway.
"I'm afraid so," she muttered.

With Bess at her heels, George reached the large,
cluttered attic. Three small windows, dusty and full of
cobwebs, let in just enough light for the girls to see
Nancy lying unconscious on the floor. They rushed to
her side.

"Oh, Nancy!" Bess wailed.

George, who was more practical-minded, felt
Nancy's pulse. "It's strong," she reported. "This is a
temporary blackout. Nancy must have hit her head."

Both girls looked around. Nearby lay a doll's trunk.
It was upside down and spread open. Directly above it
was a wide beam.

"Maybe this trunk fell off the beam and hit Nancy,"
Bess suggested.

"It doesn't look heavy enough to knock anyone out,"
George replied. "Bess, run downstairs and get some
cold water and a towel."

Bess hastened off on the first-aid errand and soon
returned with the water. George bathed Nancy's fore-

head with the wet towel. In a few seconds the young detective opened her eyes.

"Thank goodness you're all right," Bess said. "Do you know what hit you?"

"N-no," Nancy answered weakly. "Whatever it was hit me from the back."

George, sure that something heavier than the doll's trunk had injured Nancy, was searching the attic floor. Nor far from where her friend lay, she made a discovery.

"Look!" she exclaimed. "A cannon ball! I guess this is what did it," she went on thoughtfully. "It's not covered with dust like everything else up here, so it must have been inside the trunk."

Nancy sat up and smiled wryly. "I guess I'm lucky it only hit me a glancing blow."

George was angry. "Whoever put a cannon ball in a doll's trunk must have been crazy!"

Before she had time to go on with her tirade, the girls were startled to hear the stairs creak.

"Sh-h," Nancy warned in a whisper. "Let's see who's coming up."

To their astonishment no one appeared. "Someone was eavesdropping," Nancy said.

She rose and hurried to the stairway. Seeing no one, she descended quickly, with Bess and George following. Nobody was in sight on the second floor.

"Bess, run down the front stairway and find out if anyone is around," George ordered. "I'll take the back stairs. Nancy, you'd better take it easy."

Nancy needed no second urging. She was feeling very dizzy and went to lie down on her bed. Bess and George returned in a few minutes to report that no one seemed to be in the house.

"Old houses are sometimes squeaky," George remarked. "Maybe no one was on the stairs after all."

At this moment she looked at Nancy who was very white. Worried, George recommended that they call a doctor. Nancy tried to protest, but was overruled.

"Where's the phone?" George asked Bess.

"I don't know," Bess said. "Anyway, I think I should go and get Mr and Mrs Spencer."

She hurried off and in a few minutes returned with the couple. Margo Spencer, about forty years old, blonde, and attractive, was extremely concerned about what had happened. She agreed that the Drews' family doctor should be called.

"Our phone is on a table in the lower hall," she said. "I guess you didn't notice it because I always keep a large bouquet of flowers there."

George made the call, then returned to the second floor. As she started down the hall, a man came up the rear stairway. He was tall, broad-shouldered, and had thick, curly, greying hair. His eyes were deep-set and penetrating.

As he walked past Nancy's bedroom, Mr Spencer called, "Hi, Cally old boy!" He turned to the three girls. "I'd like you to meet my friend Emmet Calhoun. Cally old boy is a Shakespearean actor. Right now he's looking for another show. Meanwhile, he's helping us coach." He gave Mr Calhoun the details of Nancy's accident.

"Most unfortunate!" the actor said dramatically. "Those beautiful eyes—they might have been closed

forever!" Striking a dramatic pose, Cally old boy began
to quote a Shakespearean verse:

> " *'From women's eyes this doctrine I derive:*
> *They sparkle still the right Promethean fire;*
> *They are the books, the arts, the academes,*
> *That show, contain, and nourish all the world'*."

"Thank you," said Nancy, smiling.

Bess's eyes sparkled. "That's from *Love's Labour's Lost*,
isn't it?" she asked.

Mr Calhoun beamed. "Yes, it is, my dear. It is regrettable that most young people cannot quote from the
Bard. We can learn so much from Shakespeare."

Mrs Spencer took the actor by the arm and went
with him to the door. "Come, Cally," she said. "Let's
leave the girls alone. Nancy should rest."

The girls were a bit amused at her diplomacy. They
saw at once that Cally old boy might easily become a
bore!

"Here comes the doctor," Bess said presently. She
was glancing out of the window at the parking area.

Doctor Black examined Nancy's head thoroughly,
then said she would be all right in a few hours. "You
are to eat nothing but broth and crackers, and rest for
five or six hours," the doctor said sternly.

Bess went to the kitchen, found some soup stock, and
arranged Nancy's prescribed diet on a small tray. Soon
after eating the soup, Nancy fell asleep.

About ten o'clock that evening she awakened completely refreshed. Finding Bess and George in their
room, she announced she would like to go over to the
playhouse to see the rest of the show.

Bess and George agreed, but paused to comb their hair first. Nancy waited a moment for them, then started ahead down the front stairway. As she reached the first floor, the phone rang.

"I'll answer it," she thought, and went over to the hall table.

"Hello?" she said, just as Bess and George walked up to her.

A woman's shrill voice asked, "Is Nancy Drew there?"

"This is Nancy Drew speaking. Who is this?"

The voice at the other end, obviously disguised, cried out loudly in a cackling, witchlike tone, "I'm the dancing puppet. If you know what's good for you, Nancy Drew, you'll leave me alone. Get out! Go away!" The speaker hung up.

Nancy's expression had become one of complete amazement. When she relayed the message to Bess and George, they, too, looked stunned and worried. But in a moment all three girls regained their composure.

"Who was it, do you suppose?" Bess asked. "Some girl who plays the part of the puppet?"

Nancy shook her head. "Mr Spencer assured me that the puppet is not alive."

"It was probably the puppeteer," George guessed.

"Perhaps," Nancy conceded. "Or it might just be someone playing a joke."

"This is no joke, Nancy," Bess declared. "I think it is all part of a plot against either the Spencers or the Footlighters. Now that you're in the group, that unidentified woman is your enemy too!"

"That might be," Nancy agreed. "And it is just

possible that the doll's trunk with the cannon ball in it didn't just fall off the beam above my head."

Bess looked aghast. "You mean that someone sneaked up to the attic and deliberately knocked you out?"

"I think so," Nancy said. "And I intend to find out who it was!"

She asked the other girls if they knew whether or not there was a phone extension in the house which the "puppet" might have used.

"Mr Spencer didn't say," George answered.

The girls searched but found none. Nancy suggested that perhaps there was an extension out in the theatre, but she found that the phone in the theatre was in a booth and had a different number from the one in the house. "There's no telling where that mysterious call was dialled from," she said. "The speaker might have been nearby or at a distance."

By this time Bess was thoroughly alarmed. Grabbing Nancy's arm, she looked at her and said, "We haven't been here one night yet, and awful things are happening! Nancy, the case isn't worth it. Let's do as that caller said. Let's leave!"

·3·

An Enlightening Scene

ALTHOUGH Bess pleaded, Nancy would not consent either to leave the Van Pelt estate or to give up trying to solve the mystery of the dancing puppet.

Bess shrugged. "I suppose it's no use, but I admit I'm worried." She gave Nancy a searching look. "Probably you already have a hunch about this whole case."

Nancy laughed. "A hunch, Bess, but not one good clue."

Bess and George demanded to know what the hunch was.

"It's possible there is hidden jealousy between the pros and certain of the amateurs," Nancy told them. In a whisper she added, "I think we should watch everybody. The Spencers seem like fine people, but there may be some angle not noticeable on the surface. One of the amateurs may be trying to drive the pros out of here. On the other hand, the pros may be trying to get control and turn the theatre into an entirely professional one." Nancy suggested that the girls separate and each do some sleuthing. "Bess, suppose you keep an eye on Tammi. George, will you watch the comings and goings to the house? I'll wander round the theatre."

The girls agreed. As Nancy walked towards the big

red barn, she told herself she would phone her father and have him look up the record of each of the pros. "Maybe I'd better ask him to do the same with the amateurs," she thought.

When she entered the theatre Nancy was amazed to see how well equipped it was. On the panelled walls hung lovely paintings by local amateur artists. The stage was spacious and the scenery attractive. The audience half-filled the place. Nancy slid into a vacant seat in the last row and in a few moments became fascinated with the Civil War play in progress. Some time had passed before she reminded herself she had come to do some sleuthing. The acting had been so excellent and the play so interesting that she had completely forgotten her work.

But suddenly Nancy felt too weary to do anything but sit still. "Anyway," she told herself, "the first logical bit of detective work might be just to watch the amateur performance closely."

Presently the leading man, young Bob Simpson, walked on stage. He was about twenty years of age, very tall and dark, with darting, flirtatious eyes. After a short time, he was joined by Tammi Whitlock, who looked very attractive in her neat, trim bodice, long skirt and ruffled silk bonnet.

As Nancy watched the stage, something suddenly dawned on her. The characters were doing a love scene, which Bob Simpson was playing convincingly, yet still only as an actor. Tammi, on the other hand, was putting almost too much into the lines, and it became evident to Nancy that the leading lady was very much interested in the leading man.

"I'm sure the feeling isn't mutual," Nancy decided, as the scene changed.

The play ended soon afterwards, and the amateur performers took many curtain calls before the extremely enthusiastic audience.

Nancy made her way backstage. She was just in time to meet Bess, who whispered, "Wasn't Tammi *something* in that love scene? She certainly overplayed it. I'm glad Bob didn't fall for it. I just don't care for that girl —and I don't think Mr Spencer does, either."

"What makes you say that?" Nancy asked eagerly.

Bess reported that when the show was over, Tammi had waylaid Bob and impishly repeated some of the lines from the love scene. Bob had reddened, but before he could reply, Mr Spencer had marched up to Tammi.

"Wow! Did he bawl her out!" Bess said. "He told Tammi she was making the performance seem like a school skit!"

Nancy smiled, as she and Bess walked back to the house. One by one the actors and actresses, having changed clothes and removed their make-up, appeared in the hall. Most of them went directly to the parking area and left. Others remained to talk. Bob Simpson had been among the first to leave, possibly avoiding Tammi.

Within half an hour everyone had left. Nancy and her friends got bottles of lemonade from the refrigerator and went up to Nancy's room.

"Well, George," said Nancy, "what's your report?"

"Nothing to do with the dancing puppet," George replied. "But I have a couple of other interesting items to tell you. There was a regular battle between Tammi and Mr Spencer just before you girls came into the house. He said to her, 'Young woman, keep your personal feelings out of this theatre!"

"And what did Tammi say?" Bess asked quickly.

Her cousin grinned. "For a second I thought she was going to hit him, but all she said to Mr Spencer was, 'And suppose you stay out of *my* personal affairs!' "

Bess was thoughtful a moment, then said, "Nancy, it just might be that Tammi is a jealous person. I'm certain she has heard enough about you to be afraid you'd give her some competition with Bob Simpson, and that's why she didn't vote to have you join the Footlighters."

George laughed. "Bess, don't ever tell that to Ned Nickerson," she said, referring to Nancy's special date.

Nancy blushed a bit, then asked George what else had happened.

"I don't know if this has any significance," George answered, "but during the performance, two of the actresses came out and went into a dressing room. Pretty soon I heard one of them crying."

"Oh, what a shame!" Bess said sympathetically. "Did you find out why?"

George said the one who was crying was a girl named Kathy Cromwell.

"She's Tammi's understudy," Bess told the others.

"But she has a part in this play," said Nancy. "And she's very good, too."

"Yes, she is," Bess agreed. "But only in her own part. Every time she rehearses the lines of Tammi's part, she freezes or gets them mixed up. Poor Kathy! She's a sweet girl—not a bit like Tammi. In fact, quite shy, except on the stage."

Nancy reminded George that she had not yet told them why Kathy was crying. "Did it have anything to do with Tammi?" she asked.

"I don't know. It could have," George answered. "The only thing I heard her say was, 'I can't stand it another minute!' The girl who was with her said, 'Oh, Kathy, please—don't let her get you down!' "

Bess's eyes flashed. "I'll bet anything they were talking about Tammi. Well, I'll keep my eyes and ears open next time I'm backstage."

Nancy had already started to undress, since she had had a long and exciting day. Bess and George said good night and left her. She slept soundly and did not waken until eight o'clock the following morning. When she left her room to take a shower, Nancy discovered that the door to Bess and George's room was open.

"They must be downstairs," she told herself. "I'll hurry."

Nancy bathed and dressed quickly. She found her friends in the kitchen getting breakfast. Three good-mornings were said at once, and George added, "Ham and eggs?"

"Umm—sounds perfect!" Nancy admitted.

The three girls sat down at a large, round table in a bay window of the kitchen. They ate heartily, enjoying a few minutes' leisure, then washed the dishes and put them away.

"What's first on the agenda?" George asked Nancy.

"I'd like to investigate the theatre when no one's in it," Nancy answered.

Bess offered to straighten up their rooms. "You girls go on ahead. I'll join you later," she said.

George laughed. "You won't have to make that offer twice," she exclaimed. "I'll take sleuthing with Nancy any time to bedmaking!"

The two girls stepped out of the kitchen and walked underneath the covered arbour which led to a side door of the theatre. The arbour was used by the actors to get back and forth to their dressing rooms. Grapevines climbed lazily over the trellis, giving the walk an artistic appearance.

The barn door opened into one side of the stage, where scenery stood piled against the back wall. The opening set of the current play was already in place. Nancy and George gazed about but saw nothing unusual.

"Let's try the small barn," Nancy suggested.

They went outside and walked over to a sliding door that opened into the attached building. Inside was a small floor area with stables to the right. On the left, where the building adjoined the stage was a loft filled with hay.

Nancy's eyes fell on a ladder leading to the hayloft. "Maybe this place holds a clue to the mystery," she said hopefully. "Let's go up and see."

George followed her, and together the girls began to probe the hay. Presently George cried out, "Nancy— I've hit something!"

· 4 ·

Stage Gossip

STUMBLING across the hay, Nancy wondered what George had located.

"It's hard and heavy," George told her.

Nancy helped her friend pull the hay aside. "If this thing had been hidden much deeper, it would have fallen between the poles to the floor below," George said.

Finally the object was revealed. It proved to be a heavy wooden chest.

"This is like lead!" George remarked. She tried to lift the lid of the box but failed.

Nancy took a turn. She frowned. "There's no lock on this, but the box simply won't open."

For several minutes the girls took turns trying to pry open the mysterious little chest, without success. Suddenly Nancy said, "This reminds me of a box I once saw in the River Heights Museum. The attendant there showed me how to open the secret lock."

Deftly she felt along the back, pressing hard with one thumb. To her delight, she struck the right spot. The lid of the chest flew up!

The two girls gazed within, then looked at each other completely astonished. The box contained two small cannon balls!

"There is just space in here for a third one!" George exclaimed. "That third one must have been the very ball that hit you yesterday."

"Which would seem to prove," Nancy added, "that somebody sneaked up with it to the attic when no one was in sight, and hurled it at me."

The statement alarmed George. She began to look around fearfully and whispered, "Do you suppose anyone is hiding under the hay?"

"We'll soon find out," said Nancy, getting up from her kneeling position. "Let's take a look."

Once more the girls began kicking the hay that covered the entire loft. They found no one in hiding.

"I suppose we should remove this chest before someone else can do any damage with its contents," suggested Nancy. But the two girls found the chest too heavy and awkward to carry. "Maybe it would be better if we get that cannon ball out of the attic and bring it here to see if it matches these," the young detective decided.

"And if it does," George said, "we'll have one clue." She and Nancy hurried down the ladder and back to the house. Bess was amazed to hear what the girls had found and went with them to the attic.

"Do you think the person who threw the cannon ball is also connected with the puppet mystery?" she asked Nancy.

"I can't say," Nancy answered. "Not enough evidence to go on yet. By the way, let's not all face in the same direction in case another attacker is up here."

George stood guard at the head of the stairway, while Bess kept a sharp lookout for anyone who might

be lurking in the attic. Nancy searched for the cannon
ball.

"Why, it's gone!" she cried out.

"Gone!" the others echoed. George added, "I guess
the person who threw it is clever enough to remove any
evidence against him."

"You're right," Nancy agreed. "We'll really have to
be on our toes to catch *this* culprit!"

As the girls gathered at the top of the stairway, she
added in a whisper, "I suggest we don't go back to the
hayloft now, but watch it tonight. We may learn more
then."

Nancy further suggested that the girls should not tell
the Spencers or anyone else what they had discovered
so far. "I'd like to pick up more clues first," she said.

By noon the Spencers and Emmet Calhoun appeared,
ready for food. Margo was vivacious and humorous,
laughing about the way she kept house.

"Everything out of a can or the fridge," she said.
"Paper plates and cups on all occasions. A cleaning
woman comes every other day," she explained. "Our
hours are too uncertain for us to have a full-time maid."

Nancy smiled. "You have a well-stocked refrigerator
and pantry," she remarked. "Nobody should ever go
hungry here."

She fixed a tasty fruit salad, while Bess and George
helped Margo warm tomato soup and grill hamburgers.
Dessert was a cake from a River Heights bakery.

Conversation during luncheon was confined ex-
clusively to the activities of the theatre. There was
laughter and banter among the three professionals, and
though the girls did not understand the many in-

nuendoes that passed between the Spencers and Emmet Calhoun, they thoroughly enjoyed what Mr Spencer called "backstage gossip."

Cally old boy from time to time quoted from Shakespeare. Often he would rise from the table and speak with dramatic gestures. Once, when the conversation turned to the fact that this professional group was living on a former farm far removed from the Broadway theatre atmosphere, he quoted:

" 'And this our life, exempt from public haunt,
    Finds tongues in trees, books in the running brooks,
    Sermons in stones, and good in every thing'."

Bess's eyes had grown wide. How she wished she could act as dramatically as Emmet Calhoun! She told him this, adding, "I'm trying hard. Maybe some day I'll have a part in a play."

The actor was enormously pleased by her flattering remark. "I suppose you girls know that quotation was from As You Like It," he said.

Mr Spencer laughed. "Don't coax Cally old boy to recite too much. I think he knows every line in every Shakespearean play, and if you don't watch out, he'll be reciting them all to you!"

When the meal was over, the girls offered to tidy up. Without hesitation Margo accepted. "I really should go into town and do some shopping," she said. "There's no performance tonight, you know, so that will give me time to finish my errands."

"If you girls are looking for a job," Mr Spencer added, "there is some scenery to be painted for our next production."

"When is that show going on?" Bess asked. Secretly she was hoping she might be given a small part.

"It's supposed to start the week after next," the actor answered, "but things aren't going very well at rehearsals. I don't know what's the matter with the Footlighters. They're doing a pretty good job in the current play; but the one coming up—well, not one of the people chosen for the parts has caught on except Tammi Whitlock."

"I watched her last night." Nancy spoke up, glad to hear more about the amateur actress. "I thought she did a marvellous job."

"Oh, Tammi is talented, but she's too egotistical about her ability," Mr Spencer said. "Besides, she's a bit of a troublemaker. If she weren't so good, I wouldn't give her any part at all."

"Troublemaker?" Nancy repeated, hoping to learn more.

Mr Spencer said she was not well liked by the other actors and actresses. "She tries to lord it over everybody," he explained, "and is sarcastic and unkind in her remarks to the people who do not learn so quickly as she does."

Suddenly the girls realized that Margo was looking intently at Emmet Calhoun. She seemed to be telegraphing a message to him. Mr Spencer, feeling perhaps that he had gone far enough in his confidences, stopped speaking abruptly. Margo rose from the table and Mr Spencer and Cally old boy left the house.

When the girls were alone, Bess said "What did you make of all that, Nancy?"

"You'll be surprised when I tell you," Nancy replied.

"I have an idea Emmet Calhoun is very fond of Tammi Whitlock."

"What on earth gave you that idea?" George asked.

"A little signal that Cally old boy seemed to be getting from Margo. I thought Mr Calhoun was going to come to Tammi's defence, but Margo seemed to be warning him not to."

Bess sighed. "You're probably right, Nancy. But I'd like to bet that Tammi is no more interested in Cally old boy than I am."

The three girls worked hard that afternoon on a large piece of scenery which was to represent a tree-surrounded lake with swans floating on it. Finally paint and brushes were put away. The girls ate their supper alone, and in a low voice Nancy told of a plan she had in mind.

"Let's take my car and pretend we're going to town. We'll park it in the side road and then sneak back here to spy on the place."

"You mean watch the hayloft?" George asked.

"Yes, and," Nancy added with a chuckle, "we *may* see the dancing puppet!"

As soon as it was dark the three friends drove off. Nancy went about half a mile from the Van Pelt estate, then turned into a narrow side road. She pulled the car far over on to the shoulder, and turned off the lights.

"Somebody is coming up behind us," George remarked." We'd better not get out until the car passes."

The girls sat still.

"Duck!" Nancy ordered. "We can't risk being seen!"

They huddled together with their faces towards their

knees. In a few seconds the oncoming car, instead of passing, rammed right into the convertible.

There was a crash of glass! The three girls blacked out!

· 5 ·

Moonlight Sleuthing

FOR several seconds Nancy and her friends remained unconscious. The person who had rammed the convertible took advantage oı the time. The car reversed, then whizzed ahead.

Finally Nancy came to and raised herself up. The other car was out of sight.

"Oh, my head!" she thought, knowing she had hit the steering wheel.

Nevertheless, she turned her attention to Bess and George, who by this time were also sitting upright. "Are you hurt?" she asked.

George said she was all right—except for a lump on her forehead where she had hit the dashboard. Bess rubbed the back of her neck. "I feel as if my head were on crooked," she said, trying to be cheerful.

"How about you, Nancy?" George asked. "Do we go on sleuthing, or shall we give it up for tonight?"

"I think we'd better give up the sleuthing—at least for now," Nancy replied. "I have a strong hunch that the person who ran into us did it on purpose. There was plenty of room to pass."

George suggested that the driver might have been ill or sleepy. Nancy admitted this could be true. "In any case, I think the whole thing should be reported to Chief McGinnis."

Bess and George nodded in agreement. Before driving off, the girls got out of the convertible and inspected the damage to the car. The rear bumper needed straightening, the boot was dented, and paint was chipped off in spots.

"This is a sturdy bus," George commented. "That whack we got was enough to smash in the back of most cars."

Nancy patted the bumper. "I'm pretty fond of this old convertible," she said, smiling.

She drove directly to police headquarters in River Heights. To her delight, Chief McGinnis was there. When she reported to her old friend what had happened, the officer frowned.

"I'll send an alarm out for that crazy driver at once," he said. The chief looked intently at Nancy. "Do you have some theory as to who it is?"

"Nothing definite," the girl detective answered. "But I have a feeling that driver might have run into me on purpose—to keep me from working on a mystery I've become interested in."

"Another mystery, eh?" the middle-aged, good-natured officer asked. He had great admiration for what Nancy already had accomplished, and often told her teasingly that he hoped someday she might become a detective on his force. "I guess this case may be another game between you and me to see who'll find the culprit first!"

Since the chief's phone was ringing, Nancy had no chance to reply. She said a hurried good-bye, and the girls left his office.

Nancy drove directly to a garage in town which had twenty-four hours service. The young man on night duty had attended high school with her. She and her father considered him an excellent mechanic and always brought their car work to him.

"Hi, Joe!" Nancy called, as she drove in. "Would you have time to straighten the rear bumper on this car? Somebody out on the road got frisky and rammed into me."

Joe walked over and looked at the damage. "That's a shame, Nancy. I can straighten the bumper, but I wouldn't have time tonight to get out that dent or do any painting."

"Do what you can," Nancy told him. "How long do you think it will take?"

"Oh, an hour, maybe."

"Okay," said Nancy. "I'll go home in the meantime and pick up the car later. And, Joe—let me know if anyone brings in a car for headlight and bumper repair, would you?"

Joe nodded as the girls walked out of the service station. Nancy turned to Bess and George, saying, "We can pick up a snack at the house. I want to ask Dad to get a full report on the Spencers and Emmet Calhoun."

The girls found Hannah Gruen preparing a meal for Mr Drew, who had arrived home late and had not yet had supper. After an affectionate greeting for his daughter, and a hello to Bess and George, he asked,

"Nancy, how did you get the bruise on your head? And are you giving up your case so soon?"

Nancy's eyes twinkled. "Why, Dad, I'm here because I just couldn't stay away from you. Besides, we girls are starving. Professional actors and actresses like the Spencers don't eat much, so I miss Hannah's cooking."

Bess and George began to laugh, as they found both Mr Drew and Mrs Gruen taking the last part of Nancy's remarks seriously. "I'll get you a nice big dinner right away," the kindly housekeeper offered.

"I'm afraid," said Nancy, "that you've caught me out in a great big fib. We'll just have some biscuits—or cake—and milk," she said. "What I really came home for was to ask you, Dad, to find out all you can about Mr and Mrs Spencer and a Shakespearean actor named Emmet Calhoun, who has been staying out at the Van Pelt estate and helping to coach the Footlighters."

"I'll be happy to do that," the lawyer responded. "And now suppose you bring Hannah and me up to date on what has happened out at the Footlighters' theatre."

After the three girls had told the whole story, their listeners gaped in astonishment. "It sounds like a dangerous case," Hannah said worriedly. "Maybe too dangerous for you to continue, Nancy."

"I must admit that things have happened unexpectedly," Nancy replied, "but I think that since I've been alerted, I'll avoid letting the unexpected happen again."

Mr Drew put an arm round his daughter's shoulder. "I'm afraid, my dear, trying to do that is asking for the impossible. But I beg of you, be careful." It was now his chance to do a little teasing. He turned to Bess and George. "I hereby appoint you guardians of one Nancy Drew, detective."

"We accept the assignment," George and Bess said in unison, making low bows.

Mr Drew drove the girls back to the service station. When they reached it, they found that Joe had finished his work. Nancy thanked him for the quick service, paid him and drove off. When the girls reached the parking area of the Van Pelt estate, they were surprised to find that the mansion was in complete darkness.

"I guess the Spencers thought we were not coming back tonight," Bess remarked, as she climbed out of the car. Then, as another thought struck her, she said worriedly, "Maybe everbody has gone away and we can't get in."

"I have a surprise for you," Nancy said. "Margo Spencer gave me a key to the front door."

"Thank goodness," said George.

The girls let themselves in and went directly to their rooms. As Nancy was about to pull down the blinds at her windows, she looked out on to the dark grounds. She noticed the moon was rising.

"It will be quite light pretty soon," she told herself. "I think I'll go outside and look around for a while. Maybe the dancing puppet will perform."

Nancy left her bedside light on. She picked up a flashlight and went downstairs. Noiselessly the girl detective made her way through the kitchen and let herself out the back door.

By this time the moon had gone behind a cloud, but it was light enough for her to see the steps. Nancy went outside the trellis to a clump of bushes where she intended to hide. From this vantage point she could see the lawn and the stage-door end of the trellis. As she walked round the clump of bushes, Nancy ran full tilt into a shadowy figure!

"Oh!" she cried, startled.

Nancy instantly clicked on her light and shone it into the other person's face. "Mr Spencer!"

"Nancy! Well, for Pete's sake," the actor said. "What's the big idea?"

Nancy apologized and told him why she was there. Mr Spencer chuckled. "We had the same idea," he confessed.

"Let's watch together," Nancy suggested. "I'm hoping that as soon as these dark clouds pass and the moon lights up the lawn, we may see the puppet."

It seemed an eternity to Nancy before the black cloud had moved away. But little by little the moon began to peep from behind it. In a few moments the scene was almost as bright as daylight.

At the same instant, Nancy and Mr Spencer heard running footsteps. Looking intently ahead, they saw a girl emerge from behind the barn theatre. Recognition was impossible at this distance. The girl ran towards the road.

"Shall we follow her?" Nancy asked excitedly.

Mr Spencer grabbed Nancy's arm. "Look!" he

whispered tensely. "Over there, on the far side of the lawn!"

Nancy's eyes popped wide in amazement. "It's the dancing puppet!" she gasped.

· 6 ·

The Witch

THE life-size puppet had come out of the stage-door
entrance. It was dressed in a frilly ballet costume, and
the blonde hair was curly and close cropped.

"One thing is certain," Nancy told herself. "This *is*
a puppet, not a live person."

Mr Spencer whispered, "Now is our chance to catch
that thing!" He began to run towards the mysterious
figure.

Nancy followed and caught up with him. But before
they had gone far, the dancing puppet jerked round
suddenly and returned inside the door which slammed
shut.

When Nancy and the actor reached it, they found the
door locked. Mr Spencer looked at her. "You see what
I mean!" he cried excitedly. "It's supernatural! I tell
you, this is a ghost with a brain!"

"It certainly seems so," Nancy agreed. "How can
we get into the theatre?"

Mr Spencer said they would need a key but he had
none with him. "I'll hurry to the house and get one,"
he said. "Are you afraid to wait here alone?"

Nancy smiled. "Of course not, but do hurry!"

The actor sped off across the lawn and into the kitchen. He was gone so long that Nancy felt precious time was being lost. Finally Mr Spencer returned and unlocked the stage-door entrance. It was pitch-dark inside. He snapped on lights.

"Now where did that puppet go?" he asked, looking all round but seeing no sign of it.

"How many other doors are there?" Nancy asked.

"The only other one is the main entrance," Mr Spencer told her. They walked through the theatre to inspect it.

"Locked!" Mr Spencer said. "And bolted from the inside!"

"Then no one came out this way," Nancy said thoughtfully. "And there are no windows—the theatre is air-conditioned. Let's make a thorough search," she proposed.

Nancy and Mr Spencer looked in and behind every seat in the theatre, behind all scenery, and in cupboards. The puppet was not there.

Nancy was extremely puzzled. Aloud she said, "If I weren't so practical, I'd think that dancing figure evaporated into thin air."

"Well," Mr Spencer said, "we've lost our chance for tonight, I guess. We may as well go back to the house."

On the way, he added, "I'm glad you saw the dancing puppet, Nancy. You know now that it wasn't a figment of my imagination."

Nancy asked him if the strange apparition had ever caused any damage.

"No," Mr Spencer replied, "I can't say it has. What worries me most is that the story will leak out and people will be afraid to come to our performances."

"A few might," Nancy answered. "But a good many people might come out of curiosity. However, the only times you've seen the puppet have been late at night. Isn't that true?"

"Yes."

"Then, if I had to guess why the puppet is here," Nancy said, "I'd say it's to scare you and your wife and Mr Calhoun away from the property."

As she prepared for bed, Nancy kept mulling this thought over in her mind. It was evident that somebody was behind the strange performance. But what was the reason? And why should anyone want to frighten people out of the house? Was there something hidden there?

The following morning Nancy told Bess and George of her strange adventure and suggested that the three girls go back to the stage and hunt for a secret entrance to the attached barn.

"You think that's the only way the puppet could have been hidden from you?" George asked.

"Yes."

By ten o'clock Nancy and the cousins were standing on the empty stage gazing at the back wall. Seeing no opening, they began shifting scenery to take a look. But they found no door or sliding panel.

"Maybe there's an opening higher up," George suggested. "There might have been a ladder to it, which has been removed."

One of the props for the current Civil War play was an old farm wagon. George climbed up into it and gazed above her head. Suddenly she called, "I think I've found the door!"

The other girls climbed into the wagon and confirmed George's finding. Above them was indeed a door with an inconspicuous handle.

"You think the person with the puppet went through there?" Bess asked. "How could anybody? We can't even reach it from here."

Nancy suggested that the person might have had an accomplice to help him. By standing in the hands of one man, the other, holding the puppet, could have been lifted up to the door. "Let's try that!" she proposed.

She made a cup of her hands and lifted George high. George reached the door and opened it. "Goes into the hayloft," she told the others. She pulled herself up into it. A moment later she said, "Here's the answer. A ladder!"

She lowered it to the floor of the stage, and Nancy and Bess climbed up nimbly to join her.

"Let's pull the ladder up and put it where George found it," Nancy proposed. "We don't want to leave any trace of our having been here."

She and Bess hauled up the ladder, then Bess swung the door shut. The girls gazed around but saw no one. The puppet was not in evidence.

"It's my guess the person escaped out of this barn and went off with the puppet," Bess spoke up.

"You could be right," Nancy agreed. Then she added in a whisper, "But the puppet *may* be hidden here. Before we look, we'd better make sure no one's around."

While Bess and George walked to the edge of the hayloft and looked down, Nancy went back to see that the door to the stage was tightly closed. Suddenly the girls heard a deep voice intoning on the stage. The three stood electrified. The next moment they recognized the voice as that of Emmet Calhoun. Nancy opened the door as the actor began to quote from Shakespeare's *King Richard III.*

> " '*My conscience hath a thousand several tongues,*
> *And every tongue brings in a several tale,*
> *And every tale condemns me for a villain!*' "

Bess grabbed Nancy's arm. "He's the one!" she said. "His conscience is bothering him, and he's trying to get rid of his feeling this way!"

"Sh!" George warned, as Cally old boy went on:

> " '*O, what may man within him hide,*
> *Though angel on the outward side!*' "

Emmet Calhoun did not recite any more. He gazed around the stage, then went outside.

"Wasn't that something!" George said, chuckling.

Bess did not smile. "That's from *Measure for Measure,*" she murmured. She looked at Nancy and asked, "Do you think he's involved in this mystery?"

"It's a possibility," Nancy answered. "He *is* a strange person," she said.

George suggested that the mystery might be some kind of a joke. Bess gave her a withering look. "Joke! Nancy gets knocked on the head and somebody runs into her car?"

Nancy agreed with Bess. "One thing's sure," she said.

"We'll need a lot more clues before we can decide anything."

The girls made sure no one was hiding in the hay barn, then they began their hunt for the mysterious dancing puppet.

"Let's each take a section of the hay," Nancy proposed.

Bess and George chose the two far sides, while Nancy remained in the centre. The three girls were silent as they scuffled through the loose hay and parted it with their hands. About five minutes later Nancy's foot kicked against a hard object.

"Something here!" she sang out.

The other girls rushed to her side, and together they unearthed the hidden object.

"Another puppet!" Nancy exclaimed in amazement. "Bess, will you go and stand near the ladder and tell me if anyone comes into the barn? Nobody must know that we've found this!"

As Bess moved several feet away from the others, Nancy held up the life-size puppet. It was dressed in traditional witches' clothes.

"Who on earth hid this?" George cried out.

The others could not answer her. Nancy instantly recalled the telephone call she had received on the day of their arrival—when the high-pitched, witchlike voice had claimed to be the dancing puppet. Now she wondered if the person who had called was the owner of this witch as well as the dancing puppet.

Aloud Nancy said, "I believe we've discovered the hiding place for the ballet puppet, but we've come too late to find it."

George had a sudden idea and rushed to the spot where the chest of cannon balls had been buried. They were gone!

The girls looked at one another. "Now what?" Bess asked.

An Actress's Threat

WITH deft fingers, Nancy was already examining the witch puppet. Carefully she removed each garment and laid it on the hay.

Bess remarked, "It has a horrible face. What was the dancing puppet's face like, Nancy?"

"I caught only a glimpse of it," Nancy replied, "but I think it was more girlish. This one, you notice, has a long, sharp nose."

"Yes," George spoke up, and added, "I'll bet our detective is hunting for hidden springs or some other type of mechanism that makes this old lady work."

Nancy admitted this. The puppet was well jointed to make it execute all kinds of movements. But it had no springs, rods or levers with which to manipulate it.

"There's no sign of an opening any place," Nancy remarked.

She began to re-dress the figure. Bess kept peering over the edge of the hayloft while George, from time to time, looked down through the open door to the stage to report if anyone appeared. No one did.

Nancy, meanwhile, was mulling over the subject of the life-size puppets. Had they belonged to the Van Pelt family, or had they been brought here recently? If

51

the latter, why? Finally she finished dressing the witch and hid it under the hay in the exact spot where she had found it.

"We've searched this place pretty thoroughly," she said to her friends. "I think our next search should be in the attic of the house. There's a lot of stuff in that place we haven't examined yet."

When the girls walked into the old mansion, they found that the Spencers were just starting lunch. They greeted the girls affably, and Margo added, "*How* do you manage to get up so early in the morning? It would kill me!"

Nancy chuckled. "Just habit, I guess," she answered. "You know it's said, 'The early bird catches the worm,' and I figure if I get out early enough in the morning, I may catch a villain or two!"

The Spencers laughed, but before they had a chance to retort, Emmet Calhoun walked in. He was pounding his chest. "Nothing like a good morning constitutional," he said. "Now I'm ready for breakfast."

Since there was no food for him on the table and he did not move towards the kitchen, Bess kindly offered to fix him some breakfast. He beamed and said he would help. But before he had a chance to follow Bess, Tammi Whitlock walked into the dining-room.

"Good morning, Tammi," the others greeted her, and Emmet Calhoun gave her a wide smile.

Tammi scowled. "What's good about it?" she asked. "Well, I may as well tell you why I'm here. Mr Spencer, I want to talk to you about the next play—the one that's in rehearsal now. You know as well as I do that everything's been going wrong.

"That's because you won't take any advice. I know young people better than you do. If you don't listen to me, the show is going to be a real flop—and that will be the end of your job with the Footlighters!"

Hamilton Spencer looked stunned. The young woman's impudence held him speechless for a moment.

Tammi took advantage of the situation. With each utterance against him and the play, she became more dramatic, until she was fairly shrieking. Finally the actor rose from his chair and faced her, his eyes blazing:

"Tammi Whitlock, I've told you before to keep your personal feelings and ideas out of this theatre! I'm not afraid of losing my job. Don't forget that there must be a vote on the subject by the whole group. I admit the cast is not doing very well in the rehearsals, but your suggestions on how to run them are a lot of rubbish. Now I'll thank you not to bring up the subject again!"

Nancy and George, embarrassed, escaped to the kitchen to help Bess. Emmet Calhoun, seated at a table there, was smiling as if thoroughly enjoying the whole thing.

"I like people with fire," he said. "Tammi's beautiful when she's angry." The actor grinned. "Wish I could say the same for Hamilton Spencer." Calhoun rose in his chair, and folding his arms, quoted from *Othello*:

" 'O! beware, my lord, of jealousy;
     It is the green-eyed monster which doth mock
     The meat it feeds on.' "

Suddenly George began to laugh, saying, "We don't have to go to the theatre to see a good play. Just come to the Van Pelt house!" Her good humour seemed to break the tension that had risen.

By this time Bess had managed to burn the toast and scorch the scrambled eggs. "I'm sorry," she said. "I'll make some more."

Emmet Calhoun acted as if he had not heard her. He was gazing into the dining-room where Tammi and Mr Spencer were still battling.

With Nancy and George helping, the Shakespearean actor's breakfast was ready in a jiffy. They served it to him, then dashed upstairs.

"I think Tammi is perfectly horrid!" Bess burst out. "I don't see why they keep her in the Footlighters."

"There's one very good reason," Nancy reminded her friend. "Tammi is an excellent actress—she has amateur status, but she performs as if she has had professional training."

The three girls had just reached the stairway leading to the attic when Tammi Whitlock came hurrying up to the second floor. "Hold it!" she ordered.

The girls turned in surprise.

"Where are you going?" she asked. Nancy and the cousins remained silent. "Oh, don't act so smug," she said angrily. "Nancy Drew, I've heard you're a detective. That means there's a mystery around here, or you wouldn't be staying at the mansion."

As Tammi paused, Nancy looked intently at her and said, "Go on."

For a second Tammi seemed nonplussed, but regaining her belligerent attitude, she said, "I have a right to know what the mystery is!"

George looked at Tammi in disgust. "Assuming there

is a mystery," she said, "just what gives you the right to know what it is?"

"Right?" Tammi repeated. "Who has a better right? I'll have you know I'm the most important person in this amateur group! You and Nancy—and even Bess— are newcomers. And not one of you is an actress!" she added.

Nancy had flushed, but she kept her temper. Bess was too flabbergasted to speak. But George was furious.

"So you think you're so important?" she almost yelled at Tammi. "Well, you'd better look out or some-body will prick that bubble of conceit! You know how to recite lines and strut around the stage, but that's about it. You're a troublemaker with no respect for your elders. I could tell you a lot more, but I don't even want to talk to you. Better get out of here—and fast!"

Tammi, stunned, glared at George. She started down the hall towards the front stairway. But over her shoulder she called back, "I have influence! I'll have all three of you put out of the Footlighters!"

The girls dashed into the cousins' room and looked out the window. They saw Tammi flounce out of the house and drive off in her car. Nancy and George were ready to shrug off Tammi's threats, but Bess was worried.

"You know Tammi might try to get rid of all of us," she said. "The Footlighters can't afford to lose their leading lady, so we three might have to go instead."

Nancy had not thought of the problem this way. "If I were no longer a member of the Footlighters, I might have to leave the Van Pelt estate," she thought.

"Then I wouldn't be able to solve the mystery of the dancing puppet!"

Suddenly Bess's mood changed. "Say," she said, snapping her fingers, "I have an idea! Nancy, in school you were simply marvellous as the leading lady in plays. Poor Kathy is so scared of Tammi, she can't remember her lines as an understudy. But you could do it. Why don't you learn Tammi's lines in the present play? Then if things come to a showdown, you could take her place!"

Nancy laughed. "I could never take Tammi's place,' she said. "But I must admit I'm intrigued with the idea of learning her part. Listen, though, this must not be known to a soul but the three of us." The cousins agreed.

Nancy, who learned lines quickly and easily, began to quote from the love scene in the play between Tammi and Bob Simpson. Using George as the leading man, she overplayed the part, rolling her eyes and blowing him kisses with sighs loud enough to be heard on the first floor.

Bess, meanwhile, was so convulsed with laughter that she had thrown herself on the bed and was rolling from side to side, tears streaming down her cheeks.

"It's perfect! Absolutely perfect!" she said, dabbing her eyes.

George, too, was roaring with laughter. Finally she said, "Nancy, if you *ever* get a chance to play the part and do that to Bob Simpson, I'm telling you, Ned Nickerson will scalp you!"

"He sure would," Bess laughed. Nancy's tall, good-looking friend, who attended Emerson College, was now a summer counsellor at a camp.

Nancy grinned. "Enough play acting! Let's get on up to the attic!" she said.

At this moment the girls heard a woman's loud and terrified scream from the first floor!

·8·

The Alarming Rehearsal

"WHO was that?" Bess exclaimed fearfully.

Nancy and George did not wait to answer. The sound seemed to have come from the kitchen, so they raced down the back stairs. The girls found Margo Spencer standing in the middle of the floor, her hands over her face.

"What happened?" Nancy asked her quickly.

The actress looked at her wildly. "I saw a witch!"

"A witch! Where?" George questioned.

"Out there." Margo pointed towards the back door. "I heard a knock and opened the door. There stood the most horrible-looking witch!"

"What did she say? What did she want?" George queried.

Margo replied that she did not know. "I didn't give the witch a chance to say anything. I slammed the door and locked it."

Nancy was across the floor in two seconds. She flung open the door. No one was there! She turned questioning eyes on Margo Spencer.

"It was there! I saw it!" the actress declared. "I couldn't make up such a thing!"

By this time her husband had hurried into the kitchen. The drama coach, obviously startled, asked why Margo had screamed. When told, he began to chide her.

"How perfectly ridiculous! You're seeing things, my dear. Maybe you've been working too hard. Suppose you go up and take a nap. I'll manage the rehearsal alone."

Margo Spencer turned a withering gaze on him. "I wasn't seeing things," she insisted. "Furthermore, you have no right to question my sanity!"

"Now I know you've been overworking," her husband said gently. "I'm not questioning your sanity. We actors and actresses have great imaginations. To us, trees or bushes can take on fantastic shapes."

Margo Spencer's eyes were darting fire. Nancy felt very uncomfortable standing there. With sudden inspiration, she said:

"Mr Spencer, please let me tell you about something I discovered this morning in the hayloft. It may clarify the situation."

The Spencers looked at her in astonishment. "How?" Margo asked.

Nancy told how the hay had concealed the witch puppet. "It was well hidden and contained no strings or wires by which one might manipulate it. But it could lean against something. What you saw, Margo, might have been the witch puppet," she said kindly. "Was it standing by itself, or supported by a post?"

The actress thought a moment. "It was leaning against a post," she replied. She turned to her husband. "Now do you believe me?"

Mr Spencer made sincere apologies and gave her a kiss and a hug.

"I must go and look in the hayloft again," said Nancy. "It's just possible that the witch you saw, Margo, was not the one I found."

The whole group trooped to the hay barn. No one was around. Nancy went up the wooden ladder to the loft and rummaged in the hay.

"Our friend the witch is still here," she said. "Margo, will you come up and identify her?"

Margo climbed the ladder, followed by her husband. By this time Nancy had uncovered the figure.

"That's it!" Margo cried out. "Oh, she's so ugly! Hamilton, now do you blame me for screaming?"

Mr Spencer put an arm around his wife. "No, dear. I probably would have done the same thing."

Conversation now turned to speculation on the identity of the person who had dared bring the figure to the back door in broad daylight.

"What do you think, Nancy?" Bess asked.

Nancy laughed. "The only thing I know about him at this point is that he's fleet-footed," she replied.

She and the others made a thorough search of the theatre and the grounds but failed to find any trace of a suspect. The earth was too dry to show footprints plainly. Moreover, there had been so many people coming and going along the arbour walk that it would be impossible to distinguish the footprints of any one person.

By the time the group had finished their hunt, several girl members of the Footlighters began to arrive for the rehearsal. When they had assembled in the front row of seats in the theatre, Mr Spencer came out on the stage.

"Young ladies," he said, "I don't have to tell you that rehearsals haven't been going very well. I hope you took my last warning to heart and studied your lines carefully. I'll read the men's parts."

After taking the roll call, he went on, "The girl who was to play the part of the maid has been called out of town for a few weeks. I am giving that part to someone else—Bess Marvin!"

Bess gave a cry of delight, and Nancy and George congratulated her. Their elation was cut short by Hamilton Spencer, who said, "Everybody on stage!"

The amateur actresses took their stations in the wings, and the rehearsal began. Bess, book in hand, came on, reading her lines as the maid. In a few moments, Margo Spencer clapped her hands. Bess stopped speaking.

"Never turn your face away from the audience!" the actress told her. "And speak your lines distinctly!"

George whispered in Nancy's ear, "I'll bet Bess's knees are shaking."

Nancy nodded. "Maybe Bess is embarrassed because we're here. Let's go outside—where we can hear her but not be seen."

They had just reached the front of the theatre when Bess walked off stage. George grinned. "That *was* a small part," she said. "If we'd closed our eyes we would have missed her. I wonder if my aspiring actress cousin will come on again!"

She and Nancy went out the front door and circled round to the rear of the building, directly off the wing of the stage. There they collected the scenery still to be painted, and went to work. From what the girls could hear through the open stage door, it was evident that the rehearsal was progressing badly. The young actresses could not remember their lines and were being prompted constantly. When they did remember them, Margo or Hamilton Spencer would tell them that they were putting no spirit into the parts.

The only person on stage who seemed to be doing well was Tammi Whitlock. Nancy and George, despite their dislike of the girl personally, were spellbound by her performance.

"Tammi's good. No doubt about it," said George. "Say," she added, as a sudden thought came to her, "do you think Tammi could have had anything to do with the witch scare?"

Nancy became thoughtful. "She could have, I suppose, but I don't see any particular motive."

"I wouldn't put anything past her," George declared. "Why, she might even be at the back of the dancing puppet business!"

Nancy stared into space. George had a point! Yet Nancy felt that there was nothing to go on, so far, but a hunch. She smiled and said aloud, "My dad has always reminded me of the legal tradition, 'A man is presumed to be innocent until proved guilty.' "

The conversation of the two girls was suddenly drowned out by a tirade from Hamilton Spencer aimed at the amateur actresses.

"I'm about ready to give up," he exclaimed in exasperation.

Then Margo began to talk also. "It's hopeless, absolutely hopeless," she declared. "I'd be ashamed to have the townspeople come to such a performance!"

"The show will have to be postponed!" Hamilton Spencer announced.

At this, Tammi flew into a rage. "You mean you'll close this theatre for a couple of weeks? No, you won't! I'll see to it that you're out of here before that happens!"

"Quiet!" Mr Spencer ordered her. "You have an idea that the Footlighters cannot get along without you as leading lady in the play. Well, Tammi, you're greatly mistaken."

By this time Nancy and George were peering through the doorway at the scene inside the theatre. Most of the young performers looked as if they were ready to cry.

Tammi stood on stage, her feet planted wide apart and her face red with anger. "You get rid of me and the whole show will fall apart!" she exclaimed. "If you're inferring that Kathy Cromwell can ever take my place, you're talking like a madman!"

At this, Kathy, now seated again in the front row, began to sob. "Tammi is right," she said. "Oh, please, all of you, please stop the argument. I'm sure we can all do better. We promise to work hard. But Tammi must remain as our leading lady. I know I'm no good as an understudy. We'll just have to pray that nothing happens to Tammi, and then I'll never have to play her part."

Kathy's pleading struck home. Her friends rallied round her. Tammi stood smug, but smiling.

Finally Mr Spencer said perhaps he had been too hard on the girls. "I get carried away sometimes, forgetting you're not professionals." He begged everyone to go home and concentrate on learning the lines and gestures as he had directed.

The incident had whetted Nancy's appetite to learn Tammi's part, not for the forthcoming play, but for the one being currently produced several evenings a week. "Something *could* happen to Tammi, and if Kathy can't take her place—well, I could try."

When Bess left the theatre, Nancy asked her to get a copy of the Civil War play. Nancy closeted herself in her bedroom, and by supper time had mastered Tammi's lines in Act One.

Coming from her room, she went across the hall to speak to George and Bess. "Let's drive back to my house for dinner," she said. "I want to hear what Dad has found out about the people here."

Bess giggled. "You mean there's a chance we might have one of Hannah's marvellous dinners?" Bess loved to eat.

Nancy chuckled. "We could, of course, but there's a certain young lady who's been asked to play a part in the new show. If she gained too many pounds, she might lose her chance."

Bess considered this. Finally she said, "I won't eat dessert."

Nancy telephoned Hannah Gruen. "How nice to have you girls come to dinner!" Hannah said enthusiastically.

By the time they arrived, there was a delicious aroma of grilling steak, and macaroni and cheese coming from the kitchen.

As the group ate, Mr Drew reported that he had found the Spencers above suspicion. "They have a very fine reputation in the theatrical world."

"And what about Emmet Calhoun?" Nancy asked.

The lawyer shrugged. "So far, I have found out little about him. Seems to be a roving character. He may be harmless, but on the other hand he may not be. I suggest you keep an eye on him."

Conversation turned to the girls' adventures since last night.

Hannah Gruen was particularly interested in Tammi Whitlock. "She sounds like a tartar," the housekeeper said. Then Mrs Gruen chuckled. "I always understood that the best way to lose a boy is to chase after him!"

"You ought to see how she acts," George said in disgust. "Tammi's so bold on stage and off that it makes me sick!"

Bess kept her promise and ate none of the delicious strawberry shortcake. But she had asked to be excused from the table to avoid temptation, and was looking at a television programme when the telephone rang. She answered the call and said it was for Nancy.

"Hello," said Nancy, when she reached the phone.

"This is Joe—down at the garage," the caller said excitedly. "Say, Nancy, can you come right down here?"

· 9 ·

Shadowing

"Joe, what's happened?" Nancy asked the young mechanic.

"I have something to show you," Joe told her. "It's important!"

"I'll come right away," Nancy promised.

She returned to the dinner table and told the others about the message. Then Nancy, Bess, and George said good-bye to Mr Drew and Mrs Gruen and hurried off to the garage. When they reached it, Joe led them to a car which he said had been brought in a short time before.

"It needs front bumper and headlight work," he said significantly. "Nancy, maybe this belongs to the fellow you're looking for—the one who rammed into your convertible!"

For several seconds Nancy, Bess and George gazed at the damaged car, a recent model, black four-door saloon. Its bumper had been jammed back, and both headlights were broken.

"If the man who ran into you," said George, "is the owner of this car, how in the world did he make his getaway without headlights?"

Joe laughed. "When people are desperate, they'll

take chances. This guy probably drove off in the darkness and hid his car some place until daylight."

"I notice this car has California licence plates," Nancy remarked. "Who is the owner?"

"He gave his name as Owen Whipley," Joe replied.

"And where is he staying?" Nancy prodded.

Joe looked a bit sheepish. "He didn't say, and I didn't bother to ask. He told me he'd be back for the car in about three days. Oh, yes, he also said he was just passing through this area. Somebody got in his way, he said, and he swerved into a tree."

"Of course his story could be true," Nancy said. "But I'm going to make two tests. First, I'll back up my car and see if our bumpers are the same height from the ground."

She did this, and they came together exactly. Next, she took a magnifying glass from the glove compartment of her convertible and trained it on the front of the black saloon.

"Flecks of light-blue paint on here," she reported. "Joe, you take a look and see if you think they match the paint on my car."

The garageman made a careful examination and confirmed Nancy's suspicion that this was the car which had run into her convertible on the lonely country road.

"I'll call Chief McGinnis at once," Nancy said. "He'll probably send men here to take samples of the paint and give them a laboratory test. That's the only real way to be sure."

The chief greeted Nancy with a warm hello. He listened attentively to her story, then said, "I'll dispatch two detectives at once to make an investigation."

When the officers arrived they told Joe that he was not to permit the suspected car to leave the garage.

"Drain all the fuel from it," one of them ordered, and this was done at once.

"I guess we can't do any more now," Nancy said as the officers packed up their equipment and prepared to leave.

The three girls drove off and returned to the Van Pelt house. The evening's performance was still in progress, so they decided to go into the theatre and watch it. Noiselessly the three friends slid into seats at the back and listened attentively.

"Sounds pretty good," George remarked admiringly.

Whenever Tammi Whitlock was on stage, Nancy watched her intently. Without moving her lips, Nancy repeated the lines after the actress. She wished she dared to imitate the other girl's gestures as well, but felt she should not do this for fear of being misunderstood. However, she scrutinized carefully each movement which Tammi made.

"She's graceful and moves her body in rhythm with the meaning of the play, as a dancer does," Nancy thought.

Presently Bess smiled. She leaned over and whispered to the girls, "Kathy's magnificent tonight. You know what I think? I think Bob Simpson likes her and she's thrilled at the attention he's paying her."

George and Nancy nodded. Then George, with a low chuckle, whispered, "But watch out for fireworks from the leading lady when it dawns on her!"

As the show was drawing to a close, Nancy turned to

the cousins and said, "In connection with our mystery, I'd like to find out where each one of the actors and actresses goes after taking off the grease paint and changing out of costume."

"Okay," said George. "What are Bess's and my assignments?"

Nancy suggested that Bess hurry backstage and watch what went on there. "Maybe you'll hear some of them say where they're going."

George was to cover the dressing rooms in the house. "I'll take the special section of the parking area reserved for the Footlighters," Nancy concluded.

As the entire cast was taking bows from the enthusiastic audience, the three girls hurried off to their posts. Nancy decided to keep out of sight, and hid behind a large truck which belonged to the Van Pelt estate. It was rarely used now and not likely to be moved at this time.

As Nancy watched, she noticed that the first actors and actresses to leave the dressing rooms were young married couples.

"They're probably going home," Nancy decided.

Other performers came out alone or in couples. Among these was Kathy Cromwell, walking beside Bob Simpson. The two were laughing and looked very happy as they climbed into a car and went off together.

"Bess's hunch was right," Nancy thought.

The last person to come out was Tammi who went directly to her car. To Nancy's amazement, the leading lady seemed surprised to find a young man in the driver's seat.

"Chuck!" Tammi hissed, then added angrily, "I told

you not to come here! Suppose somebody sees you!"

To Nancy's further amazement, the stranger behind the wheel said to Tammi icily, "Shut up and get in! Remember? We have a job to do!"

As Tammi and her strange companion pulled away from the parking area, Nancy came out of hiding. She was puzzled by the remarks between the couple.

What kind of job did they have to do? Where were they going? Did it have anything to do with the mystery of the dancing puppet?

"I have half a mind to follow them!" Nancy told herself. "But it might not be safe to go alone. Oh, dear, if only Bess or George would come out!"

As if in answer to her wish, George appeared from the house. Instantly Nancy called to her, "Hurry! We haven't a moment to lose!"

· 10 ·

An Excited Patron

GEORGE sprinted across the parking area to the convertible. Nancy had already jumped into the driver's seat and started the car. Two seconds later the girls were on their way.

Nancy sped down the driveway to the main road, then stopped. She looked left and right. In the distance to her left, she saw the tail lights of a car and turned in that direction.

As she sped up the road, George asked, "What's the mad rush for? I *should* know where I'm going!"

Quickly Nancy told her friend of the conversation between Tammi and the unknown young man. George whistled. "I don't wonder you want to follow them. Sounds ominous, doesn't it?"

The car ahead was making good time, but Nancy was able to keep it in view without any difficulty. It went on and on.

Nancy did not say a word. But presently George spoke up. "We may travel for hours," she said. "Bess and the Spencers will wonder where we are."

"If we stop to telephone," said Nancy, "we may lose Tammi."

Just as she was wondering whether she should give up the chase and turn back, the car ahead turned into the grounds of a country restaurant.

" 'Green Acres'," George read the sign aloud. Then she added, "This is a very exclusive place."

"Which means we shouldn't go in without escorts— or money," Nancy said with a sigh.

"If we don't," George answered, "how are we going to find out what the 'job' is?"

"I'll park here near the end of the drive," Nancy decided. "Suppose you stay in the car so you can move it if necessary."

"And what are you going to do?" George asked.

"Scout around a little," Nancy replied. "As long as I've come this far I may as well find out what I can about the plans of Tammi and her escort!"

As she walked towards the Green Acres Restaurant, Nancy admired the fine lines of the old colonial building. Once a home, it had been converted into a fashionable restaurant. It was white, with tall pillars at the entrance and heavily curtained windows. The grounds were beautifully laid out.

"It's a lovely place," Nancy thought.

Seeing an attendant at the door, and wishing to avoid being questioned, she skirted the large wooden building. "Perhaps one of the curtains won't be drawn over the window and I can peer inside!" Nancy hoped.

To her dismay, all views of the interior were completely blocked off. "Now what am I going to do?" the young sleuth asked herself.

At this moment the dance band began to play, and

in a very few seconds a man started to sing.

Nancy listened with pleasure, one foot tapping the pavement. "Nice voice," she thought.

Just then a diner seated near one of the windows peered outside. For a few seconds he held one of the curtains open far enough for Nancy to get a good look at the interior of the dining room. At one side were the orchestra and the singer.

Suddenly Nancy gasped. The singer was Tammi Whitlock's companion! The girl detective almost laughed aloud. So this was the job he had mentioned at the parking area!

"I've certainly come on a wild-goose chase," she told herself.

Nancy was about to turn towards the driveway and rejoin George when another thought struck her. The singer who had spoken to Tammi so unpleasantly at the Van Pelt estate had said, "*We* have a job to do!" What could Tammi's job be?

"If she's singing here, then she's not an amateur," Nancy reflected. "And she has no right to be in the Footlighters!"

Nancy decided to stay at the restaurant a little longer to see if Tammi did appear in some professional act, such as a monologue or skit. The young man stopped singing, but the band continued to play.

"Maybe I should ask the door attendant about the performers," Nancy thought.

As she moved from the side of the building towards the front entrance, she became aware of a sudden disturbance at the door. Two men rushed out and dashed towards one of the parked cars.

"Hold on!" the door attendant said. "I'll get your car for you." The men paid no attention. A second later Nancy noticed a well-dressed, middle-aged woman also dash from the entrance. She was wearing a low-cut evening dress and gleaming emerald earrings and bracelets.

Pointing ahead, the excited patron cried out, "Stop thieves! Stop thieves!"

"She must mean those two men who ran out!" Nancy thought.

They had already started their car and were reversing. Quick as lightning, Nancy dashed up the driveway, calling at the top of her voice, "George, block the driveway!"

George obeyed orders instantly. She moved the convertible back so that it would be impossible for anyone to leave the grounds in a car. By this time Nancy, the woman who had been robbed, the attendant, and two other men were running after the suspects' car. When the men in it saw their escape blocked, the driver stopped short.

"Get out of the way!" he yelled at George.

"I can't," George replied, pretending that the car had stalled.

"Good old George!" Nancy thought.

In a few seconds the whole group was gathered at the entrance. The woman in the evening dress cried out to the men in the car, "You stole my emerald necklace!"

The two suspects glared at her, and the driver said, "You're crazy! We don't know what you're talking about!"

"You were right there at our table," the woman went on. "All of a sudden I noticed my necklace was gone. You *must* have taken it!"

One of the men who had joined in the chase said, "I'm James Burke, and this lady is my wife. If you're innocent, you won't object to a search."

"We most certainly do," said the driver. "Nobody except the police can search us. I tell you, we don't know anything about a necklace."

The man standing next to Mr Burke introduced himself as the owner of the restaurant. "This is most regrettable, gentlemen," he said. "But as Mr Burke has remarked, if you are innocent, then you will not mind being searched. This puts me in a very awkward position which I am sure you understand. I hope you will co-operate."

"There's no need for us to co-operate," said the driver icily. "We'll show you our drivers' licences. I think that's enough!"

He pulled a wallet from his pocket and his companion followed suit. The licences revealed that the driver was John Terrill and his friend Sam Longman. Both were from California.

Nancy, all this time, had been studying the men closely. The driver was slim in build and dark, while his companion, Longman, was stockier and had unruly, light brown hair. They both looked about thirty-five years of age, well-to-do, and did not seem like criminals.

Nancy wondered what would happen next and whether George would be forced to move the convertible. At that moment a car came whipping up the road and turned in. It stopped dead upon reaching the blockade.

"Police!" Nancy thought in relief. Two officers jumped from their car and approached the group.

"How do you do, Mr Landow?" one of them said to the restaurant owner. "Some trouble here?"

Quickly Mr Landow explained what had happened. When Mrs Burke kept insisting the two men had taken her valuable emerald necklace, the officers said they would make a search. Grudgingly the two suspects permitted this. The necklace was not found on either of them.

"We'll look in your car," one of the officers said, and a thorough search was made inside the vehicle. The necklace did not come to light.

"I hope you are all satisfied," said John Terrill. "You can be sure, Mr Landow, that not only will this be the last time I patronize your restaurant, but I shall tell everyone I meet not to come here! As for you, Mrs Burke, you ought to have your head examined for making such a scene. And now, if somebody will move that convertible out of the way, we'd like to leave."

The officers also looked at the men's driving licences, then let them go. George deftly moved the car and the Californians rode off.

Nancy addressed the restaurant owner. "Does a young woman named Tammi Whitlock work for you?"

The man shook his head. "I don't know such a person," he replied.

"She's in the restaurant now," Nancy went on.

"Then she's a patron," Mr Landow answered. He turned away and walked back to the restaurant with Mr and Mrs Burke.

The police followed, saying they would make a thorough search of the restaurant to see if they could locate the stolen necklace. Nancy did not wish to intrude, but she was interested in learning when and how Mrs Burke had missed her jewellery. The young detective ran to catch up with her.

"Pardon me, Mrs Burke," she said, smiling, "but I was wondering if perhaps I might help you." She chuckled. "I have a reputation for being able to find lost objects. I don't mean to intrude in the police search, but would you mind telling me what happened just before you missed your necklace?"

Nancy's manner was so straightforward and she was so attractive-looking that no one in the group took offence at her request. Mrs Burke stopped and said, "Well, my husband and I were seated at a table not far from the dance floor. When the singer, Chuck Grant, left the platform he came right past our table. I liked his looks and the way he sang, so I smiled at him. He stopped to chat.

"At that moment the two men who just left here also stopped at the table. One stood behind me and the other beside me. They began to kid Chuck Grant, and the conversation went on for several seconds. Then all three left.

"Right after that, I missed my necklace. It hadn't fallen to the floor, so I was sure the man who stood behind me had taken it."

Nancy told herself that any thief who could have

done this without attracting attention must indeed be amazingly adept.

Mr Burke added, "My wife became very excited and started running after the two men. They also started to run. I must admit it made them look guilty." He sighed. "But you saw what happened."

"Where did Chuck Grant go?" Nancy asked.

"Oh, he had walked off in another direction. I believe he was sitting at one of the tables with a young lady."

"Tammi!" Nancy thought. For a fleeting second she wondered if there could be any possible connection between Tammi, Chuck and the two men. But instantly she put the idea out of her mind. It was too improbable!

"Well, thank you for telling me," said Nancy. "I must go now. A friend is waiting!"

As the two girls left the grounds of the Green Acres Restaurant, Nancy told George the whole story. "Instinct tells me this journey wasn't a complete waste of time," she added.

"And instinct tells me," said George, "that in view of what happened last night on the road, we'd better roll up our windows and lock the doors."

"You're right," Nancy agreed.

There was only moderate traffic on the road and the girls came within sight of the Van Pelt estate without interference. Nancy heaved a sigh of relief and turned into the driveway. But a moment later she jammed on her brakes. There was a roadblock of sawhorses across her path.

"Well, for Pete's sake!" said George.

She was about to get out and remove the horses,

which she recognized as part of the theatre's stage props when, without warning, brilliant lights were flashed into the two girls' eyes from each side of the convertible!

· 11 ·

The Incriminating Mark

NANCY and George blinked in the strong glare of the bright flashlights.

"Roll down your windows!" a man's voice ordered.

Nancy paid no attention to the order. George too remained adamant.

Although the girls' eyes had not become entirely accustomed to the light, they could vaguely make out that the persons holding the flashes were masked men. Nancy was sure that the one who had spoken was trying to disguise his voice.

"I said roll down your windows," he warned.

Instead of obeying, Nancy put her hand on the car's horn. She held it down, and in the stillness of the night it reverberated loudly.

"Stop that!" the man on her side ordered.

Nancy paid no attention. But after she felt sure the alarm must have been heard, she took her hand off the horn. Nancy did not touch the window, but called through it, "Why did you stop us?"

"Because we want to ask you a few questions," the masked man replied. "You didn't have to call for help. We're not going to hurt you."

Nancy waited for him to go on. He looked across the

top of the car and the girls could see the other man nod. Finally the one alongside Nancy said, "Why are you girls snooping around this place?"

He received no answer. The girls kept watching the men closely.

"You're cool customers," said the masked man who was doing the talking. "But you won't keep so cool if you stay here. I'm warning you that the Van Pelt estate is a dangerous place. The sooner you get out, the better."

"And if I don't choose to go?" Nancy countered, hoping that help would soon be coming from the house.

"You haven't seen anything yet around here," the stranger went on. "The theatre, the house and the grounds are haunted!"

Nancy and George almost laughed. One moment the speaker sounded like a hoodlum, and the next he was talking like a frightened child about the place being haunted. There was a pause, with no one saying anything. Suddenly the girls became aware of running footsteps.

"Help at last!" thought Nancy. She tooted her horn a couple of times.

She and George held their breaths, wondering what the men would do. To the girls' relief, the two intruders suddenly took to their heels and dashed down the road in the direction of River Heights. The engine of a getaway car started with a roar just as Mr Spencer, Emmet Calhoun, and Bess came running up. Nancy and George rolled down the windows.

"Why the roadblock?" George demanded, leaning out the window.

"Who put these here? What's going on? Where have you been?" Mr Spencer cried excitedly. "You girls had us scared to death."

"Tell you later. We were stopped by two masked men who just left here," Nancy replied.

"What!" Bess cried. "How frightening!"

"It was no joke," Nancy agreed. Briefly, she explained what had happened. "Did you set up the road-block, Mr Spencer?"

"No. The men must have taken these props from the theatre."

Bess sagged limply against the side of the car.

"Oh, Nancy, George, what a narrow escape you had!" she gasped.

Mr Spencer and Emmet Calhoun thought they should not let the two masked men get away. They started to climb into the convertible and Mr Spencer said, "Nancy, we'll chase them!"

To his surprise, Nancy did not move. With a slight smile, she said, "This time I picked up a clue. I know who one of the men is."

The others looked at her in astonishment. George asked, "How could you? They were masked."

"Did you recognize his voice?" Mr Spencer questioned.

Nancy shook her head. "George and I had a little adventure up at the Green Acres Restaurant—tell you all about it later. But the important thing is, two men suspected of being thieves were stopped there and searched. They were allowed to go because a stolen necklace was not found on them."

"Yes, yes, go on," Bess pleaded.

"One of those men," Nancy continued, "had an unusual scar just above his right wrist."

George blinked and asked, "And you mean to say the masked man who was standing beside you here had a peculiar scar above his right wrist?"

"I certainly do," Nancy answered. "His name is John Terrill. He's from California and the police have this data."

"Nancy Drew, you're an absolute whiz," said Bess.

The two men looked at her admiringly and praised her fine sleuthing. Nancy felt sure that in some way John Terrill was connected with the mystery at the Van Pelt estate. But she said nothing, not knowing whether or not Emmet Calhoun knew of the mystery of the dancing puppet.

"I'd like to phone Chief McGinnis at once," Nancy said.

Mr Spencer and Emmet Calhoun removed the sawhorses and carried them inside the theatre. In the meantime, Nancy drove to the house. She asked George to park the car while she made the phone call.

"Chief McGinnis," she said, when he came on the line, "have you a few minutes to talk to me?"

Receiving an affirmative reply, Nancy related the whole story—from the time she had seen Terrill and Longman run out of the restaurant to the moment the holdup men had dashed away in a car from the Van Pelt estate. On purpose, Nancy said nothing about Tammi or Chuck Grant, the singer. She would pursue that little mystery on her own!

"It looks," Chief McGinnis remarked, "as if those men were determined to keep you from interfering in anything further they may want to do. I'll alert my men to keep an eye out for Terrill and Longman. They could possibly be the same elusive fellows who've pulled similar daring jewel thefts lately in this area. You say the local police searched the restaurant and grounds thoroughly?"

Nancy said she did not know that exactly, but she was sure the men had not thrown the necklace any place outdoors. "I was watching from the instant they came out of the door. The police had not yet searched the inside of the restaurant when I left. Maybe they found Mrs Burke's necklace afterwards."

Chief McGinnis asked Nancy to hold the line a moment. He himself went to another line and called the police in the town nearest the Green Acres Restaurant. The report came back that the necklace had not been located on the floor or among the linen tablecloths and napkins used that evening at the restaurant. The Burkes had finally gone home, saying they would report the loss to their insurance company.

"Nancy, that was a very good night's work on your part," said Chief McGinnis. "And now I have something amazing to tell you. I was talking to Joe, the garageman, about the car which we think rammed yours."

"You mean the one driven by Owen Whipley?" Nancy asked.

"Yes," the officer answered. "But what do you make of this? Owen Whipley, according to Joe, has a peculiarly shaped scar just above his right wrist!"

Nancy was thunderstruck. "Really? Is it something like the shape of a crawling snake?"

"Exactly, I don't have to tell you, Nancy, that Owen Whipley and John Terrill are probably one and the same person."

"Do you think," Nancy asked, "that John Terrill is his right name, or is it Owen Whipley?"

Chief McGinnis said it was too early in the case to determine this. "Both might be aliases, and the man might even be using forged licences."

"And what about his friend Sam Longman?" Nancy queried.

"I wonder myself. It's a mix-up all right," the chief admitted. "Call me again any time, day or night, if you pick up another clue."

Nancy promised to do this. By now Bess and George had come into the house. Babble and excitement started all over again. Margo Spencer arrived from upstairs in robe and slippers to hear what had happened. Bess and George fixed a snack for everyone, while Nancy retold her story.

As soon as they had finished eating, she escaped to her room, weary and full of questions. When puzzled, Nancy liked to stretch out on the bed in the darkness and think things through. Right now she was extremely curious about Terrill, or Whipley, whichever his name was. Why was he interested in trying to get her away from the Van Pelt estate?

Before she had a chance to start undressing, there was a tap on her door.

"Nancy?" She recognized Mr Spencer's voice.

Nancy opened the door. In a whisper, the actor said, "I'm going outside to watch for the dancing puppet. I have a feeling she'll show up again tonight. If she does,

I'd like to let you know so you can be there."

"But she'll be gone by the time you warn me," Nancy objected.

Mr Spencer grinned. Reddening slightly, he said, "I've rigged up a bell system from the kitchen to your room." He pointed to a crude arrangement on the bedside table.

Nancy chuckled. "You think of everything. Yes, I'd like to be notified if you see the dancing puppet. I'll sleep with my ears wide open!"

Mr Spencer said good night and went off. Nancy closed the door and soon was ready for bed in shortie pyjamas. As she turned out the light and rolled up the window blind, the young sleuth thought, "The moon will be up late tonight, but it's a perfect setting for a ghostly performance."

At that moment there was another knock on her door, and Bess came in. "I know you must be dreadfully tired," she said. "But I can't resist telling you something. In the show tonight, Tammi pulled another one of her overdone love scenes with Bob Simpson. And that's not all. He left the theatre as soon as possible and literally ran towards his dressing room in the house. Tammi dashed after him. I had gone on ahead and saw this, so I hid behind a bush and watched. She said something to him—I couldn't hear what it was—but he started running faster than ever, and called over his shoulder, 'Don't be silly!' "

Nancy burst out laughing. "I hate to say it, but it served Tammi right." Then she became serious. "Tammi had quite an evening. First being ditched by Bob, then finding a man in her car whom she acted surprised to see and apparently had to go off with."

"This place is full of surprises," said Bess, yawning. "Just now I came past Emmet Calhoun's room. The door's open. He isn't there, and his bed isn't turned down!"

Nancy was amazed to hear this. "It's a funny time of night for him to be going off," she said thoughtfully. "Come to think of it, he wasn't with us in the kitchen when we were having a snack. Where could he have gone? He doesn't have a car."

"Search me," Bess said. "Well, good night."

When Nancy finally settled down, she thought she would go over the chain of events in the mystery. But sleep overcame her immediately. She was deep in slumber when her subconscious mind became aware of a tinkling sound.

The newly rigged bell on her bedside table was ringing insistently!

· 12 ·

Puppet Snatcher

IN a moment Nancy was wide awake. Thinking it best
not to turn on the bedroom light, she felt for the chair
near the window on which she had laid the dress she
had worn that evening. She pulled it over her head.

As she stepped into sandals, Nancy gazed out of the
window. Her heart began to beat faster.

*In the centre of the lawn, a life-size puppet in ballet costume
was jerkily dancing across the grass!*

To Nancy's amazement, a flashlight was trained on
the figure. The light came from some bushes along the
driveway leading into the estate. Nancy could not see
the person holding the light.

"I must hurry!" she told herself, and although it took
only a few seconds to zip up her dress, it seemed like an
hour to the excited young detective. She grabbed her
own flashlight and dashed along the hallway towards
the back stairs.

"Cally old boy isn't in yet," she told herself, noting
that his door was still open and the bedcovers still in
place.

As Nancy leaped down the stairway, she wondered
about the Shakespearean actor. Had he disappeared in
order to put on the puppet show?

A moment later she reached the kitchen, sped across it and out of the door. At the foot of the steps, partially concealed by the bushes, stood Mr Spencer. Nancy went to stand beside him.

"It's unbelievable!" he whispered in an awed tone. "Nobody's working that puppet, yet it acts as if it were human!"

Nancy strained her eyes to see if she could figure out any explanation for the movement of the jerky, yet at times graceful, motions of the dancing puppet. She could see nothing to indicate wires or string. Could it have a mechanism inside which was wound up?

"We must capture the puppet!" Nancy declared. "Come on!"

With no pretence at moving stealthily, the two dashed across the grass. By this time the mysterious figure was not far from the trees where the flashlight shone on it.

"We're gaining!" Nancy thought in delight. Any moment now she might solve the mystery surrounding the dancing puppet!

Suddenly the bright flashlight ahead went out. For a few seconds Nancy and Mr Spencer could not see the dancing figure, but as soon as their eyes became accustomed to the pale moonlight, they detected her still dancing jerkily across the lawn.

Nancy doubled her speed. She was still some distance from the puppet, when suddenly she was startled to see a long-robed, black-hooded figure emerge from among the trees. The person, with his back to her, reached out and grabbed the dancer. Tucking her under his arm, he made a wild run for the road and disappeared in the darkness.

"Good heavens!" Mr Spencer cried out, trying to catch up with Nancy.

The heavy line of trees and bushes along the curved driveway had swallowed up the puppet and her abductor. Nancy followed doggedly. At the point where she reached the driveway, it curved ahead sharply. The black-hooded figure was not in sight. Nancy hurried round the bend. Still no sign of the mysterious person.

"Where did he go?" she asked herself. She listened for the sound of a car but heard none. "He must be escaping along the main road."

Nancy dashed all the way to the end of the driveway and looked up and down. The dancing puppet and the person carrying her were not in sight.

Before going farther, Nancy decided to wait for Mr Spencer and see what he had to suggest. The actor, when he caught up with her, was out of breath and disgusted. He felt there was little more they could do. "We can train our flashlights among the trees," he said. "The fellow may be hiding."

Nancy and the actor made a thorough search casting their lights behind every tree and bush. Their quarry was not behind any of them.

"He made a clean getaway," said Mr Spencer. "I suppose we may as well go back to the house and get some sleep."

Intent on searching the ground, Nancy did not reply.

Mr Spencer went on, "I don't mind confessing to you, Nancy, that this puppet business has me extremely worried. It was bad enough when just the dancer was involved, but now that we know there is a flesh-and-blood puppeteer who doesn't want his identity known, I'm more worried than ever. Have you any theory?"

"Just one, Mr Spencer. We haven't yet learned why the puppet is made to perform, but I'm sure the reason is one that involves another mystery."

"Oh, dear!" Mr Spencer sighed.

Suddenly Nancy found what she had been looking for—the footprints of the hooded figure. She pointed them out to the actor.

"Here are some deep, well-formed prints," she said. "I'll ring them with stones and then ask Chief McGinnis to send men out here to take casts of them."

"You mean in the morning?" the actor asked, and Nancy nodded.

He helped her find some small stones, and they encircled several of the footprints.

Mr Spencer heaved a sigh, then chuckled. "You certainly *are* a detective, Nancy," he said. "I'm delighted your father suggested that you help me solve the mystery of the dancing puppet."

"Better save your thanks until I really do something," Nancy replied, smiling, as she and Mr Spencer started back to the house.

As Nancy began to drop off to sleep once more, she could not help wondering again about Emmet Calhoun. She had meant to ask Mr Spencer where he was, but had forgotten to do so.

"Oh well, I'll find out in the morning."

There was no further disturbance that night, and everyone slept soundly. As usual, the Spencers were not up when Nancy and her friends came down to break-

fast. While Bess was scrambling eggs, Nancy telephoned Chief McGinnis and told him about the circled
footprints.

"Very good, Nancy," he praised her. "I'll send a
couple of men out there to take casts."

"I'll meet the officers at the gate," Nancy offered,
"and show them the exact spot. What time will they be
here?"

"Nine thirty," the chief replied.

Promptly at that hour Nancy was at the entrance
gate of the Footlighters' property. When Officers Jim
Clancy and Mark Smith arrived, she led them to the
spot where she and Mr Spencer had carefully laid the
small stones.

Footprints and stones were gone!

Thinking she had made a mistake in the location,
Nancy searched for further footprints similar to those
she had ringed. There was not a sign of one of them!
The two police officers, holding the equipment they
had planned to use, stood in silence watching her.
Finally she admitted that the footprints had been removed.

"The person who made them must have come back
and brushed them all away, Indian style, with tree
branches," she remarked.

The officers did not comment, nor give any sign that
they thought she had brought them out on a wild-
goose chase. They knew Nancy Drew by reputation
and felt sure she would not purposely report a false
alarm to the police department. They helped her
search.

"Probably," said one of the men, "the fellow came

back here in stocking feet. He sure doesn't want you to find out who he is."

"Nor the police," Nancy added.

Suddenly she turned her gaze upwards among the trees. "I have a theory. I believe the man we were chasing last night climbed one of these trees and overheard everything Mr Spencer and I said."

"You're probably right," said the other officer. "Well, Jim, I guess we may as well go back to headquarters."

"Wait a minute!" Nancy pleaded. She was not ready to give up yet, and furthermore she wanted to compensate for having called them on a futile errand.

Quickly she began examining the tree trunks in the area where she had found the deepest footprints. Presently she exclaimed, "This trunk looks as if the bark had been newly peeled off!"

Before the two officers could reach the tree to verify her statement, Nancy began to climb the trunk. Soon she was lost to view among the branches. A few seconds later the men heard her cry out.

"What is it?" one of them called up.

Nancy's excited voice came back. "I've found a clue!"

· 13 ·

A Surprising Command

"I'VE found the hiding place of that puppeteer!" Nancy exclaimed from her perch in the tree.

"What's up there?" asked Officer Clancy.

"Wait until I pick up the clues. I'll show them to you." Nancy replied.

There was silence for a minute or two, then Nancy started down the tree.

"Will you catch these—and please be careful of them," she called to the men below.

Through the air floated a piece of black cloth, a jagged square of grey suiting, and several bits of pink tulle.

"What in creation are these?" Officer Smith asked in amazement.

When Nancy reached the ground she explained. "The man we were trying to catch last night wore a long black-hooded robe. I'm sure this is a piece torn from it. The grey one is from his suit."

"But he certainly wasn't wearing pieces of pink net," Officer Clancy spoke up.

Nancy grinned. She was pretty sure these men knew nothing about the dancing puppet. For this reason, she merely answered, "Chief McGinnis will understand.

Please give these to him. Have you something in which to wrap the pieces?"

"Yes," Officer Clancy replied, "in the car."

Officer Smith opened the door and brought out a waterproof bag. He dropped the evidence into it and promised to take the bits of cloth at once to Chief McGinnis.

"Please ask him to let me know if he tracks down the owner of the grey suit," Nancy requested.

"Righto," Officer Clancy said, as the men started to drive off.

Relieved that a valuable clue had made the officers' visit worth while, Nancy returned to the house. She entered the kitchen, smiling broadly.

At once Bess and George wanted to know what had happened. "You haven't caught the villain, have you?" Bess asked teasingly.

"I wish I had, but I did find a piece of his suit and his black robe. The puppet left a clue too. I sent the police a piece of her tulle skirt."

As Nancy paused and sniffed the aroma of muffins in the oven, George said, "Don't stop there. Go on with your story."

"Tell you what," said Nancy. "I'll trade the whole story for a good breakfast."

"It's a bargain," said Bess, giggling, as she opened the oven door and took out a tray of blueberry muffins.

"Umm, they look delicious," said Nancy, and helped remove them from the tray to a warm plate.

Soon the three girls were seated in the dining-room enjoying sliced oranges and bananas, crisp bacon and muffins. Nancy had just finished briefing her friends on what had happened while the police were there, when Emmet Calhoun stalked into the room.

"Good morning, ladies," he said jovially. "Prithee, fair maidens, extend a hungry man a crust to lift his spirits."

The three girls chuckled and invited him to sit down. Bess said she would get some oranges and bananas for him.

"Aren't you up pretty early for an actor?" George needled him. "Especially for someone who stayed out all night?"

Emmet Calhoun blinked. "You knew I was away?" When George nodded, he went on, "Friends from town phoned that they had news of a possible role for me in *King Richard III* and would pick me up late, I stayed with them overnight, but in order to get a ride back, I had to come early."

The girls looked at each other. So Calhoun had been practising when they had heard him reciting alone on the stage. The actor offered no further explanation, but arose and began to pace the dining-room.

"Ah, 'thereby hangs a tale,' as 'tis said in *The Merry Wives of Windsor*." He paused dramatically. "I had a most delightful night in town. Good fellowship, good food, good music. It was as if life's troubles had vanished.

> " '*Why, then the world's mine oyster,*
> *Which I with sword will open.*' "

"Ah, yes," Calhoun went on. " '*We have some salt of our youth in us.*' "

Despite Nancy's slight suspicions of this man and his unawareness of how much trouble he might be to other people, she was amused by him. His quotations were apt, and his manner of delivery was convincing. Nevertheless, she wanted to find out if there were more to his activities of the night before than visiting friends, and whether he knew anything about the puppet or the puppeteer.

"Parties in town are fun," Nancy said. "But I love the country with its wide-open spaces and fields and flowers and trees. Oh, I feel bad every time I see a beautiful tree being cut down." Then she in turn quoted:

> " 'And many strokes, though with a little axe,
>   Hew down and fell the hardest-timbered oak.' "

Emmet Calhoun's eyes opened wide, and he looked at Nancy with admiration. "Excellent. I see you know Shakespeare's *Henry the Sixth*." Before Nancy could reply, he went on, "Did you ever think of training for the theatre? You have a marvellous speaking voice. Think about it, my dear. You might become a great actress!"

Nancy beamed and blushed a deep red. Bess and George looked at her. They wanted to tell Emmet Calhoun that at their request Nancy had become a self-appointed understudy for Tammi Whitlock. But they said nothing.

"Trees, ah yes," Emmet Calhoun went on. "I love trees, but if you must know a little secret, I am scared to death of climbing one!"

Nancy could not decide whether the actor was telling

the truth, or whether he might have been disguised as the black-hooded figure and had made the remark deliberately to throw her off his trail. She remembered that Emmet Calhoun had worn a grey suit the evening before.

But somehow, the Shakespearean actor, though eccentric, did not strike Nancy as being dishonest. Maybe I should direct my suspicions elsewhere, the young detective thought.

After breakfast Nancy told the cousins she was going to learn Tammi's lines in Act Three of the Civil War play.

"What about Act Two?" Bess asked her.

"I think I've almost mastered them," Nancy answered. "There aren't so many in that act, if you recall. That's where Kathy is rather prominent, and Bob Simpson too. He's marvellous in that scene with the President, isn't he?"

"He certainly is," said Bess. Then she asked, "No sleuthing today?"

"Oh, yes," Nancy answered. "But give me two hours to rehearse first. Then I think we should make another search of the attic for clues to the dancing puppet mystery."

At the appointed time she was ready. The three girls had just reached the foot of the attic stairs when Emmet Calhoun approached them.

"Going to the third floor?" he asked.

"Yes."

"I'm sorry, but you can't do that," he told them.

"Why not?" George spoke up.

Calhoun told them that only the officers of the Footlighters were allowed in the attic. "In fact, no one else in the club is supposed to go above the first floor."

George declared firmly, "Mr Spencer invited us here, and we can go anywhere on these grounds that we wish!"

Calhoun smiled patiently. "Not according to our leading lady, you can't."

"Tammi!" George cried in a tone of disgust. "What does she have to say about it?"

The actor shrugged. "Since I'm not a member of the Footlighters, I am not familiar with the club's rules and regulations. All I know is, Tammi asked me to promise that if anyone went up to the attic I would let her know at once."

"Well, of all the nerve!" George exploded. "It's high time somebody taught Tammi Whitlock a lesson!"

Nancy laid a hand on George's shoulder. "Take it easy," she said. "I'll phone Tammi myself and get not only this matter but a few more things straightened out!"

Nancy hurried downstairs, looked up Tammi's number in a list of members of the Footlighters, and put in the call. It was answered by a gentle-voiced woman who said she was Tammi's aunt.

"Please call my niece later," she said. "Tammi was out late last night and is still asleep. I don't want to disturb her."

Nancy did not know what to do. She was sure the woman was telling the truth. Yet she wanted to find out whether or not the girls were allowed to investigate the attic of the old Van Pelt mansion.

While she was thinking what to say, Tammi's aunt

went on, "My niece must be rested and in good form today. She has a rehearsal of the next show this afternoon and then the regular performance tonight."

"I see," Nancy replied. Since she had already thought of another way to obtain the information she wanted, Nancy told the woman she would be in touch with Tammi later and hung up.

Nancy now looked at the list of members again and dialled the business number of the Footlighters' president. His name was Bill Forrester, an affable man who gave a great deal of time to help make the whole amateur project a success. When Nancy told him what she had heard and asked if it were true that only the officers of the club could go above the first floor, he laughed.

"Tammi is a fine little actress," he said, "but she certainly pulls some funny ones. At a recent meeting of the executive committee of the Footlighters, she proposed a motion that only the president, the secretary-treasurer and herself could have access to the rooms above the first floor, other than regular occupants of the mansion. The rest of us didn't see any sense in this, so she was outvoted."

"Then it's all right if I go up and look around the attic?" Nancy asked, relieved.

"Go ahead," Bill Forrester replied. "But don't forget, if you find any treasures they belong to the Footlighters."

"Of course," Nancy said, laughing.

She returned to the second floor, where Bess and George were still arguing with Calhoun and making it plain to him that they did not care for Tammi Whitlock. He, in turn, was defending her.

When Nancy told of her conversation with Bill Forrester, Calhoun shrugged. Then, striking a dramatic pose, he quoted from Shakespeare's *Troilus and Cressida:*

"'My mind is troubled, like a fountain stirr'd; And I myself see not the bottom of it.'"

He walked off and went down the front stairs. Nancy and her friends hurried to the attic. Bess posted herself at the top of the stairs, while Nancy and George began a hunt through the dusty boxes and trunks set under the eaves.

The two girls worked for some time but did not find a single clue to the mystery of the dancing puppet. George had just closed the lid of a carton and started to open the trunk next to it when suddenly something flew up into her face!

· 14 ·

Nancy's New Role

As George cried out, Nancy ran quickly to her side. Bess, too, left her post to come and find out what had happened.

The next second all three burst into laughter. A large jack-in-the-box had risen up and smacked George on the cheek!

"Well, this place doesn't lack surprises," she said ruefully, rubbing her cheek.

The girls gazed at the jack-in-the-box. It was a toy clown fastened in a wooden chest about a foot square and was well constructed. "An expert made this," Nancy commented. "I wonder if it could have any connection with the puppet."

She examined the jack-in-the-box thoroughly but could find no similarity to the witch figure in the barn. "Let's continue our hunt," she suggested.

"I guess I'd better get back to my post," said Bess, and she returned to the top of the stairway.

Nancy and George were intrigued by the contents of the trunk. It contained a crude set of hand puppets and a miniature stage with a long curtain draped below it to hide the puppeteer.

"I just can't get it out of my mind that there is a tie-up between the old Van Pelt family and the present mystery of the puppet," said George.

"If you're right," said Nancy, "no doubt the mysterious puppeteer has found some clue to a valuable possession of the Van Pelts' and is trying to find it."

"You mean," said George, "that he is using the dancing puppet to scare people away from here so he can hunt for it?"

"Possibly," Nancy answered. The thought of Tammi and her latest move to keep the girls out of the attic occurred to her. Was Tammi in some way connected with the mystery? Were she and Emmet Calhoun in league with each other?

For the next half hour the three girls took turns guarding the stairway and searching the other trunks, boxes and cartons. They came across nothing suspicious.

Finally Bess said, "It's way past lunchtime and I'm starved. Let's get something to eat."

At that particular moment Nancy was staring at the far wall of the attic. She began to walk towards it, saying, "I have a hunch there's a hiding place up here that we haven't found yet. Wait until I examine that wall."

It took several minutes' close scrutiny of the old wooden wall to find a concealed latch.

"Here it is!" Nancy said, excited at the prospect of what she might find.

George started to walk towards her, while Bess remained at the top of the stairway.

Nancy had a little trouble discovering just how the latch worked, but in a few moments she felt it turn. Gently she started to pull and a door opened.

Suddenly she became aware of a movement inside the cupboard and the next second the life-size puppet of a Pierrot stepped out! As Nancy stared in astonishment, the puppet's left arm, which had been held upright, was lowered menacingly.

"Oh!" screamed Bess.

George leaped forward, but Nancy had already dodged out of the way. The three girls watched fascinated as Pierrot continued to walk jerkily straight ahead. After it had taken several steps, the figure turned and crashed into a trunk. It fell over with a clatter.

The next instant Bess called out, "Here comes Cally old boy!"

"He mustn't see this!" Nancy said tensely. She and George grabbed the puppet, dragged him back to the cupboard, and just managed to close and latch the door when Emmet Calhoun appeared at the top of the stairs.

"What crashed?" he asked.

George gave a loud laugh. "Haven't you ever noticed how clumsy I am?" she asked.

The actor received no further explanation. Instead, Nancy said to him, "Have you ever been up here before?"

Emmet Calhoun shook his head. "I detest attics. They're usually full of spiders and dust and make me sneeze."

The girls grinned, and Bess added, "I haven't sneezed yet, but on the other two counts I agree with you." She showed smudges on her slacks.

"These trunks contain lots of interesting old things," Nancy said. "But nothing too unusual." She did not add that there were three boxes of books which the girls had not examined. "We're all starving, and we're just about to go down for something to eat. Would you like to join us?"

"That would be delightful," Calhoun replied, and followed the three girls down to the kitchen.

While Nancy washed lettuce for a salad, she said to him, "We found a big Jack-in-the-box and some hand puppets in one of the trunks. Are you interested in puppets?"

"No more than the average person," Calhoun replied, "though I have read a good deal on the subject." There was no sign that he was not telling the truth.

Nancy thought, "I didn't get anywhere with that lead," and suppressed a smile.

"Has it ever occurred to you," the actor asked, "that people are really puppets in this world? As Shakespeare says in *As You Like It*:

> " '*All the world's a stage,*
> *And all the men and women merely players.*
> *They have their exits and their entrances;*
> *And one man in his time plays many parts.*' "

Bess spoke up. "I don't know much about puppets. When did they come into vogue?"

Emmet Calhoun said they were one of the most ancient forms of play acting. In the days of the Greek and Roman theatres they were used in plays. "And in this country the North American Indians used puppets in their ceremonies," he added.

Emmet Calhoun explained that there had been little

change in the method of making puppets perform since the early days of their use.

"And there's a fascinating story about how marionettes came into vogue in Venice in the year 944," he went on. "Toymakers there fashioned tiny figures of brides which they called 'little Maries'. When the French toymakers imitated them, they changed the name to marionettes. By the way, did you know it is thought that Shakespeare's plays *Midsummer Night's Dream* and *Julius Caesar* at one time were performed by marionettes?"

The three girls admitted that they had never heard this. Emmet Calhoun also told them that during the reign of Queen Victoria in England, puppets were made larger than ever before. At times, he said, they were used on the stage with live actors.

Nancy asked the actor if he had ever heard of a puppet or marionette being worked in any other way except by strings. Calhoun shook his head. "I don't see how they could be," he said.

Nancy was satisfied now that Emmet Calhoun knew nothing about the dancing puppet, the witch or the Pierrot which she had found.

As the group was finishing lunch, Margo and Hamilton Spencer walked into the kitchen. They said hello, then at once began to speak of their distress over the forthcoming play.

"Those amateurs have got to work hard in the rehearsal this afternoon," Mr Spencer declared severely. "Bess, do you remember your lines and gestures?"

Bess looked a little frightened. "I—I think so," she faltered.

The whole group went over to the theatre, and one by one the young actresses straggled in. Some of them had jobs but had managed to get a few hours off from business.

Nancy and George sat in the front row. Soon all but Tammi had arrived. Mr Spencer, not to waste time, took sections of the play in which she did not appear and coached the other players.

Suddenly he walked out on to the stage, his face red with anger. Stalking up and down, he said, "What's the matter with everybody? We can't put on a performance like this! You say the lines, but you don't put any vitality into them!"

"I'm sorry," Kathy Cromwell spoke up. "It's hard for me to act natural when I'm supposed to be talking to a man—and a girl is reading his part."

"That's no excuse!" Mr Spencer shouted. Then he thought better of his remark. "I'll play the part myself." He walked over and took the proper position on the stage, telling Kathy to come on and start again. This time she played the role very convincingly.

"Maybe there's something in what you said," he conceded. "We'll have to have more full rehearsals together. Tonight *everybody* will stay after the show and go through the lines for this play."

There were groans from the girls, and the coach was reminded that it would be about three o'clock in the morning before anyone would get home.

"Well, I'll decide after I see how you make out this afternoon," Mr Spencer said. "By the way, is Tammi here yet?"

"No," George called up to him.

Tammi Whitlock never did arrive for the rehearsal. Finally Nancy told Mr Spencer of her conversation with the girl's aunt. "Apparently Tammi expected to come," Nancy said.

Suppertime drew near and still there had been no word from Tammi. Mr Spencer announced that he was going to telephone her house.

George, her eyes sparkling with an idea, followed the actor. She stood off at a little distance while he made the call. It was easy to guess what was being said on the other end of the line. Tammi's aunt was telling Mr Spencer that she had tried to phone, but found the line busy. Her niece had lost her voice completely and would not be able to perform that evening!

Mr Spencer put down the phone and sat staring into space. George knew what was running through his mind—what was he going to do? Kathy simply was not ready to take on the part which Tammi had been playing!

George walked up to the actor. "I couldn't help overhearing your conversation," she said. "Perhaps I have a solution to the problem."

Mr Spencer stared at her. "A solution?" he repeated.

"Yes," said George, and she told him how Nancy had learned Tammi's lines in the play. "She has been rehearsing in secret and imitating every gesture of Tammi's."

"That's astounding," said Mr Spencer. "Are you recommending that I put Nancy on tonight, when she's never been over the part with the rest of the cast?"

George smiled. "That's up to you, of course," she

said. "But I suggest, before you turn down the idea, you go through the lines with Nancy herself."

Mr Spencer, ready to grab at a straw to save the situation in which Tammi had placed him, agreed to do this. "Go and get Nancy and meet me on stage. I'll take Bob Simpson's part."

When George made her announcement to Nancy, the young sleuth was stunned. "Why, George——" she began.

"I think that's a simply marvellous idea!" Bess spoke up. "Come on, Nancy!" she urged.

With trepidation, Nancy and the cousins hurried out to the barn theatre. Mr Spencer met her, holding a Civil War ball gown in one hand and a wig with long curls in the other.

"Put these on," he directed, "and see how they fit."

Excitedly, Bess and George went into a small room at the side of the wings with Nancy and helped her into the costume.

"You look simply radiant!" Bess said admiringly.

Nancy's heart was pounding as she walked towards the stage. She turned and said to her chums, "Wish me luck!"

· 15 ·

Curtain Call!

GEORGE held her breath as Nancy began speaking her lines. Mr Spencer, taking the part of Bob Simpson, gave no sign that he was either pleased or displeased with Nancy's performance.

Whenever there was a scene between the leading lady and another girl character, he called Bess to read the lines. "But don't do any acting," he said.

George, now seated in the auditorium, kept her fingers crossed. She noticed that the only time Mr Spencer stopped Nancy was to drill her on stage directions. Nancy spoke the lines without once forgetting them, and imitated Tammi's movements to a point where George at times could hardly keep from chuckling.

The rehearsal went on and on. Presently an idea came to George. She left the theatre but returned about twenty minutes later. She was smiling and saying to herself, "Nancy will certainly be surprised."

Presently Mr Spencer said he wouldn't need Bess to read the lines any longer, so she came down to sit beside George. In a few moments the two girls quietly went out together.

Nancy thought, "They've gone to cook supper, I'll bet."

She herself felt a slight pang of hunger, but she was too excited about the rehearsal to pay further attention to it.

"I suppose I should give you a breather," said Mr Spencer finally. "Nancy, I didn't want to say anything before, but now I will admit to you that I am absolutely amazed at your ability. I had heard that you performed very well in school plays, but I had no idea you could do this well."

Nancy smiled. "Don't forget I've been watching Tammi intently and trying to imitate her."

"Well, you've certainly done a remarkable job. Now, if you're ready, I'd like to go over the scene where you're seated on the couch reading a letter and Bob Simpson comes in unexpectedly to bring bad news. Please be very intent while reading the letter. Then, as you become aware of his entrance, start to rise and let the letter flutter to the floor."

As Nancy crossed the stage towards the couch, she thought, "That's not the way Tammi does the scene. Mr Spencer must think his way is better. I wonder if her personal interest in Bob made her interpret the scene differently."

Nancy went through the lines and motions exactly as she had been directed, and Mr Spencer smiled his approval. "Please be sure to do it just that way to-night. It was perfect."

Three more short scenes were rehearsed, then Mr Spencer looked at his watch. "My goodness, it's seven o'clock!" he said in amazement. "Nancy, will you

please take a warm shower to relax, have a short rest
period, then eat a very light supper. Tell Margo I'll be
in shortly."

Nancy delivered the message, then went to the second
floor. Surprised to find that Bess and George were not
around, she returned to the kitchen to ask Margo
where they were.

"I don't know," the actress replied. "But I did see
them go off in your car."

Wondering where the cousins had gone, Nancy returned to her bedroom, took a shower and lay down for
twenty minutes. Then she went to the kitchen. After
eating a sandwich and drinking a cup of tea, Nancy
went over to the theatre. Bess and George still had not
returned.

"Where could they be?" Nancy wondered.

The cousins, meanwhile, had hurried to the River
Heights airport. George, thinking that Nancy's father
and Mrs Gruen, and also Ned Nickerson, would like
to see the performance that evening, had telephoned
Mr Drew. Then she had called the camp where Ned,
Burt Eddleton, who was her own favourite date, and
Dave Evans were counsellors. All of them told her they
would like to see the show. The boys would come by
plane.

"I hope it's on time," Bess fidgeted, as they sat waiting. "We'll just about get back to the theatre in time
for the curtain."

Over the loud-speaker they heard the plane's arrival
being announced. The girls hurried to the gate, ready
to whisk the boys off as soon as they came through it.
Ned and his friends, realizing what a tight schedule

they had to meet, ran all the way from the plane to the gate.

"Hi!" five voices said at the same time, and everyone laughed.

"The car's over here," George explained, leading the way. The trio of college boys formed a most attractive group: Ned, tall and athletic, with brown hair and blue eyes; Burt, blond and a little shorter than Ned; and Dave, rangily built, with dark hair and green eyes.

"So Nancy's trying to solve another mystery—with the help of you girls," Ned said, as the car spun along the road.

"It's a weird one this time," George answered. "But I don't know how much we're supposed to tell, so perhaps we should wait and let Nancy do it."

"Fine thing!" Burt complained. "After all the help we fellows have given Nancy on other mysteries!"

"Yes," Dave added, "think of all the miles we've travelled and you won't even let us in on the excitement."

Bess and George knew they were being teased, but still refused to divulge any details about the mystery of the dancing puppet.

When the young people walked into the theatre, Mr Drew and Hannah Gruen were already there in seats next to those for the newcomers. Greetings were quickly exchanged.

"Sh!" George whispered. "Curtain time!" Mr Spencer was walking out to the footlights.

He announced that Tammi Whitlock was suffering from laryngitis and would be unable to play her part that evening. "The Footlighters are very fortunate in having obtained the services of Nancy Drew."

As the curtain went up, Bess and George glanced round the theatre to see what the reaction was to the change in leading ladies. Some of the audience looked surprised, others frowned. The girls felt that many residents of River Heights had heard what an excellent actress Tammi was and had purchased tickets just to see her.

But as the play progressed, the applause for Nancy between acts became genuine. The young sleuth seemed to have become inspired in the part.

Bess and George were seated together, with their dates on either side of them. Bess now whispered to her cousin, "I'm glad Nancy isn't overplaying the love scenes with Bob Simpson the way Tammi does."

George suppressed a chuckle. "But look at Ned's face," she whispered. Ned Nickerson sat with a grim jaw and eyes straight ahead. He leaned forward slightly in his seat as Bob kissed Nancy. When the scene was over, he heaved a sigh and sat back, drumming his fingers on the chair arms.

As the final curtain came down, the applause was thunderous. All the members of the cast had played their roles unusually well, hoping to support Nancy as best they could. There was curtain call after curtain call, with Nancy and Bob Simpson commanding a major share of the crowd's enthusiasm.

Mr Drew was among those who were clapping the loudest. Hannah Gruen's eyes were moist.

"I didn't know Nancy was that good!" said Dave. "Boy, she ought to make the stage her career."

"And give up sleuthing?" Bess exclaimed. "She wouldn't do it in a million years!"

As soon as the audience began to leave, Bess and George took the others to the house. Nancy, waylaid several times and offered congratulations, had not yet taken off her Civil War costume or her wig. Suddenly she saw her father and Mrs Gruen, who promptly hugged her. Then, over Hannah's shoulder she saw Ned, Burt and Dave.

"Well, for goodness sake!" she cried. "Oh, it's wonderful to see you! But how in the world did you get here?"

"Flew in, at George's invitation," Ned said quickly. "Nancy, you were simply great. I didn't have time to pick up a bouquet for you, but you deserve it. About five dozen red roses!"

After Burt and Dave had congratulated Nancy, Ned went on, "I think this calls for a celebration. How about all of us going out somewhere together?"

"Thank you," said Hannah Gruen. "But I think I'd better return home." Mr Drew also said he should get to bed since he had to be up very early the next day.

Nancy was silent. "Well, how about it?" Ned asked her.

She blushed, then said she was greatly embarrassed. Bob Simpson had asked her to go out with him and she had accepted.

Bob had just come from his dressing room and overheard the conversation. He walked up, smiling. "I couldn't help overhearing what you said, Nancy. I know these fellows have come a long distance. I'll be glad to step down—that is, if you'll give me another date."

Suddenly an idea came to Nancy. "Ned, do you and Burt and Dave have to go back tonight?"

"Yes, we do."

"Then I have a suggestion. We girls will have to drive you out to the airport, and it will be late coming back alone." She smiled at Bob. "It might be good for us to have a male escort."

The leading man grinned. "Well, if you insist. But how about my finding a date? Maybe I can talk Kathy into going."

"Swell idea," said Ned.

Bob had seen Kathy leaving the house alone. Now he rushed after her and was just in time to invite her to go with the group. The two came back together and Kathy appeared to be delighted.

"I'm honoured to be included in the celebration for our new leading lady," she said.

Nancy laughed. "I assure you this is only temporary. As soon as Tammi gets her voice back, I'll stick to painting scenery!"

"You'll do nothing of the kind," said Kathy. "I don't mind telling you that Tammi and I aren't the best of friends. I wish you'd keep the part."

Kathy went into Nancy's dressing room with her and helped her change into street clothes.

"It's too bad that you and Tammi don't get along," said Nancy. "I'm going to ask you a very blunt question. Is it because of Bob Simpson?"

Kathy nodded. "Tammi is absolutely hateful to me. Of course, you've already guessed she's crazy about

Bob, but I certainly didn't take him away from her. If he wants to date me, why shouldn't he? Nancy, do you know that Tammi actually *threatened* me?"

"Threatened you! In what way?" Nancy asked her.

Kathy said that Tammi had forbidden her to make dates with Bob. "She said if I did, she'd see to it that I never got another part in a play!"

"You didn't take her seriously?" Nancy asked.

"I tried not to," Kathy replied. "But she gets me so upset I forget lines and never do my best when she's around. One night I actually cried because of what she'd said."

Nancy put a hand on Kathy's shoulder. "You must try hard not to pay any attention to Tammi. I admit I don't understand that girl myself."

Kathy said she felt better and was sure her acting would improve from now on. "I won't let Tammi get me down—either on the stage or in real life," she said firmly.

As the girls left the dressing room, Mr Spencer came up. He announced that the evening performance had gone so well that there would be no rehearsal that night for the next play.

The young people climbed into Bob's car. "Where to, ladies?" Ned asked.

Nancy, her mind reverting to the unsolved incident of the stolen necklace at the Green Acres Restaurant, suggested that they go out there. "They have a good dance band and a young singer named Chuck Grant. I think you'll like the place."

George chuckled. "Last time we girls were there, we didn't go inside. Nancy and I thought we had nabbed a couple of thieves, but the loot wasn't on them!"

"One thing is sure," said Bess. "Those two suspects won't dare show up there again."

"Why not?" Nancy countered. "So far they've proved their innocence to the authorities, and they don't suspect I recognized one of them by the scar when he stopped my car."

Ned gave Nancy a searching look. "Something tells me you still suspect them of the theft. Am I right in guessing that you think they may have had a confederate in the restaurant and that's why the necklace wasn't found on them?"

Nancy laughed. "Mind reader!"

When they entered the restaurant, the headwaiter showed the group to a table at the edge of the dance floor. Soon the four couples were enjoying the lively dance rhythms. After a short intermission, the band returned to the platform. This time Chuck Grant came on stage and sang.

As soon as he finished, Chuck stepped down from the platform and came directly to Nancy's table. "You're Nancy Drew, aren't you?" he asked. When Nancy nodded, the singer went on, "I hear you were absolutely terrific in the show tonight."

Nancy looked amazed. "Thank you," she said, smiling. "Where did you hear that?"

"From several guests who have come in since the performance," he replied. "I think I ought to warn you—Tammi Whitlock is not going to like the report. She's a firebrand when she's jealous!"

Nancy laughed. "Tammi has nothing to worry about. Her role is waiting for her whenever she can come back to take it." Then, wishing to change the subject, Nancy asked, "Where'd you learn to sing so well?"

"California," Chuck Grant replied.

Nancy recalled that Tammi came from California. "Then you knew Tammi out there?" she inquired.

Chuck Grant threw back his head and laughed heartily. "I'll say I did. Don't you know who she is?"

· 16 ·

Aliases

CHUCK Grant leaned towards the waiting group. "Tammi Whitlock is my sister!" he startled them by saying.

"Your sister!" George repeated. "Well! *That* explains a lot of things."

"What do you mean?" the singer asked quickly.

George was on her guard at once. "Oh, your ability in the arts," she replied. "And one night we saw you leave with her from our theatre."

"I see," Chuck answered. Had Nancy imagined it, or did the young man look relieved?

"Where did you pick up the name Chuck Grant?" Ned spoke up.

The singer said that Chuck was a nickname. His family had great objections to his singing with bands in restaurants. "So I took the name Grant." He chuckled. "When I was a little boy I fell in love with a movie star. Her name was Lola Grant. The name has brought me good luck—here in the East."

"Did Tammi come here because you did?" Nancy asked him.

"Sort of," he replied. "I came because a friend of mine lives here, and I stay with him. Tammi's with our aunt, but that's too slow for me!"

Bess giggled. "Slow! Even though you work in a place like this?"

Chuck said that the management was very strict, and he was not allowed to make dates with any of the patrons. "So if I weren't staying with a friend, I probably wouldn't have met anybody around here or had any fun," he explained.

Nancy asked him how often he saw Tammi, and he said about once a week. "To tell you the truth," he confessed, "my sister and I don't agree on a lot of things. She treats me too much like a kid brother."

Nancy smiled, and then said, "I understand there was a bit of excitement around here the other night when a Mrs Burke's valuable necklace was stolen. Did she ever find it?"

"Not that I know of," Chuck answered. "But then I wasn't too interested and didn't pay much attention."

"Did you know the two men who were accused of taking the necklace?" Nancy prodded him.

The young singer stared at her, frowning. "I don't know what you mean. Why should I know a couple of crooks?"

"Of course you wouldn't," Nancy said with a disarming smile. "I heard that you and the two men happened to stop at the Burkes' table at the same time, that's all."

"Oh, if *they're* the accused men, I never saw them before in my life," Chuck answered. "Mrs Burke—if that's her name—smiled at me as I came off the platform. She seemed like a nice motherly soul and I was feeling kind of lonesome that evening, so I stopped to chat."

At this moment the band began to play again. Chuck excused himself and returned to the platform. Nancy and her friends got up to dance.

When they returned to the table, Ned looked at his watch and said, "Much as I hate to break up this party, we fellows must catch a plane. I think we'll have to go now." He summoned the waiter and asked for their bill.

From time to time Nancy had glanced over the patrons in the restaurant, hoping that the two suspected men might come in. But they did not appear.

"If those two are thieves, they probably work their racket in a different place every time," she thought.

Soon she and her friends were in the car speeding towards the airport.

"It's been a swell evening," Ned declared, as the boys were ready to show their tickets at the gate and walk out to the waiting plane. "And listen, Nancy, you watch your step solving this mystery. Promise me, if you do need any help, you'll give me a call."

Burt guffawed. "You'd need a magic carpet to get here in time to do any good!"

Dave also put in his gibe. "If I were you, Ned, I'd tell Nancy to stay away from the stage before she starts taking her lines too seriously!"

The banter continued until the three girls, Bob Simpson, and Kathy Cromwell said good-bye to the visitors and waved as they boarded the plane. The Footlighters group stayed to watch the take-off, then Bob took his new leading lady and her friends back to the Van Pelt mansion before he drove Kathy home.

Although it was late, George and Bess followed

Nancy into her bedroom and talked excitedly about the whole evening—how marvellous Nancy had been in the show and how surprising Chuck Grant's announcement was.

"Do you think," George asked, "that Tammi and Chuck are in league about something?"

"If they are, there's no clue yet as to what it is," the young sleuth answered.

Bess yawned and remarked, "He called Tammi a firebrand. I'd like to bet that you'll hear from her about playing her part so well tonight."

George grinned. "Tammi can't do anything until she gets her voice back! I hate to wish anyone hard luck, but I hope she doesn't recuperate too soon!"

The next morning, just as the girls finished eating their breakfast, the telephone rang. Nancy answered it. The caller was Chief McGinnis.

"I have some news for you, Nancy," he said. "We've picked up a suspect in that necklace job."

The chief requested that Nancy, Bess, and George come down to headquarters. The suspect was to be put in a line-up for identification. The girls arrived promptly and were introduced to a stranger, named Mike Besser, a pawnbroker in a town some distance away. Among the assembled witnesses was Joe, the garageman.

The group was given seats in the main room of police headquarters. Then six men were marched in by an officer and ordered to turn so they would face Nancy and the others.

Not a word was spoken until Chief McGinnis said to the group, "Have any of you ever seen any of these men before?"

At once Mr Besser spoke up. "That fourth man from the left is the one who came into my shop and pawned an emerald necklace."

"Did you notice anything unusual about him?" the officer went on.

"No, I didn't," the pawnbroker replied.

Joe now answered the chief's question. "That same man—the fourth from the left—he's the one who brought in the car with the smashed headlights and bumper."

Bess whispered to Nancy, "The one who rammed into your convertible!"

Nancy and George had been watching the accused man intently. Now Nancy spoke up. "He's one of the two men we saw at Green Acres Restaurant! He was suspected of having taken Mrs Burke's necklace."

The other men in the line-up were excused. The suspect was brought by the policeman to face the watching group at closer range. Nancy whispered to Chief McGinnis, "Will you ask him to pull up his right shirt sleeve?"

The prisoner refused, so the policeman did it for him.

"There's the scar!" Nancy cried out. "I'd know that scar anywhere!"

The prisoner gritted his teeth and looked balefully at the group in front of him, but he said nothing. Chief McGinnis explained that when the man had been found in his apartment, he had papers on him showing that he was Owen Whipley.

"That's the name he gave me," Mr Besser spoke up.

"And me," Joe nodded.

Nancy looked at Chief McGinnis. "But at the Green

Acres Restaurant he had a driver's licence made out to John Terrill!"

The officer faced the prisoner. "Which is your right name and which is an alias?" he asked him. The suspect did not answer.

"We'll make him talk later," said the chief, and ordered the policeman to take Whipley to a cell and lock him up.

The officer thanked Mr Besser and Joe for their co-operation. When the two men had left, Chief McGinnis turned to the girls and said, "Nancy, I want to thank you for your tip. My detectives kept working until they found a tailor who had a jacket with a hole in it to be woven. The grey fabric exactly matched the snip you found in the tree out at the Van Pelt estate."

"And did you find the dancing puppet and the hooded robe too?" Nancy asked eagerly.

Chief McGinnis shook his head. "No, he apparently keeps them somewhere else."

Just then the police guard who had taken Whipley away returned. He reported that the prisoner still claimed he was being held illegally—that he had committed no crime.

"Whipley claims," the policeman went on, "that some unknown person helped himself to his car and dented it. Whipley took it to the garage to be repaired. As for the stolen necklace, Whipley insists he knows nothing about it. He says the one he took to the pawnbroker belongs to a relative who was hard up for cash."

"His story about the car accident has been changed completely," Nancy remarked.

Chief McGinnis smiled. "Whipley's explanations

sound pretty flimsy. We'll hold him until he can find some proof to back up his statements."

Before leaving, Nancy asked Chief McGinnis where Whipley had been living.

The officer grinned. "I know you'll pick up a clue," he said. "Whipley has been renting an apartment at 24 Ambrose Street."

The three girls went to that address in Nancy's convertible. Two young women with prams were talking in front of the apartment house.

Nancy stepped from the car and went to speak to them. First she admired the two adorable babies in the prams. Finding the young mothers friendly, she asked:

"Do you happen to know a Mr Owen Whipley, who lives here?"

"I know him," one of the young women answered, "but he doesn't live here. He has an apartment round the corner."

Nancy looked surprised. She said, "Do you happen to know John Terrill?"

"He lives here," the other woman replied.

Nancy laughed. "I'm certainly confused. I thought they probably lived together." She did not want the two women to suspect she was fishing for information.

Apparently they were unaware of her probing. One said, "If you want to find Owen Whipley, he's at 16 Dayton Avenue."

"I know where that is," said Nancy. "I'll just stop here a minute and see if Mr Terrill answers his bell."

She went inside the apartment house and looked at the mailboxes. Not finding either the name Whipley or Terrill, she went over them all again. Neither was listed, but there was one box without a name. Apparently the suspect did not wish anyone to call on him!

"I suppose the police got their information through the superintendent," Nancy thought, as she came back outside.

She waved to the two young women and climbed back into her car, then set off for 16 Dayton Avenue. On the way she told Bess and George the latest development.

"What a mix-up!" said Bess.

"Maybe the man who called himself Sam Longman at the restaurant is now using the name Whipley," George remarked.

"Or," Nancy added, "maybe Terrill rents two apartments."

Bess sighed. "This mystery is getting beyond me. All I know is that two men using three names are from California, and so are Tammi Whitlock and her brother. Say, do you suppose Chuck Grant was just giving us a story and isn't her brother at all?"

"Your guess is as good as mine," Nancy answered. "My only hunch right now is that Owen Whipley or Sam Longman, or whoever he is, won't answer his bell."

In a few minutes she parked, and the girls entered the rather shabby-looking apartment house at 16 Dayton Avenue. It proved to have no lift, and Nancy noted that again there was one mailbox without a name on it.

"It probably belongs to the man we want to see," said George. "Come on! Let's go up!"

Nancy laid a restraining hand on her chum's arm. "We have no right to make a search," she said. "I think we should get in touch with Chief McGinnis, tell him what we've found out, and ask him to send a couple of detectives here to go upstairs with us."

There was a public telephone on the wall near the front door. Nancy put in a coin and called the chief. Speaking barely above a whisper, she told him her findings and he promised to send men over at once. Upon the arrival of the officers, who introduced themselves as Foster and Dougherty, she led the way to a rear apartment on the third floor.

They rang the bell and waited excitedly. There was no answer. Then Detective Foster knocked. Still there was no answer, but Nancy's sharp ears caught the sound of a movement inside the apartment.

"I'm sure someone is in there," she whispered to the officer. "I have a suggestion. It may or may not work. Possibly these thieves use passwords of one sort or another. You might try saying 'Green Acres' and see if it works."

The detective nodded. He tapped on the door lightly and called, "Green Acres! Green Acres!"

Within seconds the group heard footsteps, and a man opened the door. The startled occupant took one look at the visitors and tried to slam the door. When Detective Foster prevented this, the man took to his heels through the apartment.

"That's Sam Longman!" Nancy cried, recognizing him as Whipley's companion at the Green Acres Restaurant.

The girls and the detectives rushed after the suspect.

By this time Longman had reached a bedroom. He banged the door shut and locked it.

Suddenly Nancy exclaimed, "There may be a fire escape off that room! He'll get away!"

"No, he won't!" said Detective Dougherty. "Foster, you and Miss Drew run down and stop him. I'll break down this door!"

·17·

The Chase

As Detective Foster and Nancy rushed from the apartment house, they almost collided with a woman hovering over a baby in a pram. A tall, husky man stood beside her.

Foster stopped, opened his coat to show his detective badge, then commandeered the services of the man. "We're after a suspect, and I may need help," the detective said.

Nancy, meanwhile, had asked the woman if there was a fire escape from the left side of the building. The young woman nodded, saying, "You can get on to it from every floor through a bedroom in the rear apartments."

The detective, the other man, and Nancy sprinted into an alley. Nancy pointed. "There he is! Just jumping down from the foot of the fire escape!"

The three pursuers doubled their speed but were not able to lessen the gap between them and the fugitive.

"He mustn't get away!" Nancy cried out.

To the men's amazement, she was more fleet-footed than they. Nancy had vaulted a fence which the suspect had jumped over, and was now running down an alley towards the next street.

The detective and the other man finally caught up

with her at the street. Longman was weaving his way to the opposite side, dodging traffic.

"Stay here!" Foster commanded Nancy.

At that moment a red light on the nearby corner stopped all traffic, giving the two men a chance to dash across the street. After a short chase up the block, they nabbed their quarry! He was putting up a fight, Nancy observed, flailing his arms and trying to wrench free.

Longman soon found it was useless to fight, and accompanied the men to the corner. At a green light they all walked across to where Nancy was waiting.

"We'll go back to the apartment," said the detective. He turned to the stranger who had helped him. "Thank you for your assistance. Here comes Detective Dougherty. He'll take over."

The stranger gave a quick salute, said he had been glad to help, and walked off. The others returned to Longman's apartment.

Detective Foster told everyone to sit down in the somewhat shabby living-room. To Longman, he said, "Now talk!"

The prisoner began to bluster. "What's this all about? You have no right to hold me! I haven't done anything!"

"If you won't tell your story," said Detective Dougherty, "suppose we ask you a few questions. Do you know that we have located the emerald necklace you stole at the Green Acres Restaurant?"

Longman glared at the detective. "I don't know what you're talking about."

"What is your real name?" Foster pursued the interrogation.

When the man refused to answer, Nancy spoke up. "I know two names he uses, but maybe neither one is his real name. One is Owen Whipley, and the other is Sam Longman."

Suddenly the prisoner, his eyes blazing, cried out, "Who's this girl, anyway? What right's she got to question me or say who I am?"

Quietly Bess spoke up. "Nancy Drew is a detective—and a very good one too!"

Dougherty now told Longman that his pal, John Terrill, who also used the name Whipley, was behind bars. Longman gave a visible start and looked frightened. Then his bravado returned, and he said, "Well, that's his hard luck!"

The officers tried in various ways to get the prisoner to say more, but he merely continued to protest his innocence. Finally Dougherty asked Foster to guard him, while he made a search of the apartment.

"It's against the law!" screamed Longman.

Dougherty pulled a search warrant from his pocket. Then he and the three girls began a really intensive search for evidence. Every cupboard and bureau drawer was investigated. Twenty minutes later the searchers were ready to admit defeat. They had arrived in the kitchen as the last area in which to hunt. Longman, a self-satisfied smirk on his face, was standing in the doorway with Foster behind him.

"You're nuts if you think you're going to find anything here," he bragged.

Cupboards were opened. They revealed a few dishes and several cans of food—nothing more. Discouraged, the searchers stood in the centre of the room, while Longman watched, grinning.

"What did I tell you?" he said. "Now get out of here, all of you!"

Suddenly Bess had an inspiration. She dashed across to the gas cooker and opened the large oven door. The eyes of the other searchers popped in amazement.

Jammed inside the oven was the missing dancing puppet!

"For Pete's sake!" Dougherty cried out. "What's this?"

To the astonishment of the two detectives, Nancy explained that this figure had been seen dancing eerily around the Van Pelt estate. "My friends and I have been trying to solve the puppet mystery," she said.

Everyone now turned towards Longman. Foster asked him, "Where'd you get this, and what's all this about having a dance on the lawn?"

"I'll tell you nothing," the prisoner answered, "except to admit that my friend and I have used the name Whipley as an alias."

Nancy spoke up. "Then at least one of your drivers' licences is forged?" she guessed, and Longman nodded.

By this time Bess had carefully lifted the puppet from the oven. It was carried into the living room and set on a straight chair. Nancy began to examine the figure in its frilly dress. Now was her chance to find out how the puppet worked!

Longman's eyes had narrowed almost to slits as he watched the girl. Presently Nancy said, "Oh, the whole back comes off!"

"What's inside?" asked George. Before Nancy could reply, Longman jumped towards her and screamed frantically, "Don't touch that! You'll be electrocuted!"

All eyes turned on Longman. "I'm an electrician," he continued. "That puppet is highly mechanized and works by remote control to electric wires. There's a live one inside. If you touch it, it'll be curtains for you!"

"Oh, Nancy!" Bess exclaimed. "You might have been killed!"

Nancy seemed less ruffled by Longman's announcement than the others in the room. If there were a live wire, it had been put there for a reason. "I'll bet," she thought, "that Sam Longman has something hidden inside this puppet he doesn't want us to find!"

She communicated her idea to the others. The suspect glared at her.

Detective Dougherty looked at Nancy in admiration. "You are probably right. We'll look inside this puppet, but we won't take a chance. I'll call the police electrician to handle it with the proper tools."

He told Foster to go down to their car and radio Chief McGinnis. The detective made the call and within a short time Smitty, the police electrician, arrived. He admitted that Longman's statement was partly true and it was just as well that Nancy had not put her hand inside the back of the puppet. Smitty unhooked wires leading to strong batteries.

"Once upon a time this puppet worked by being wound up," he announced. "There's a sturdy spring here, but the key has been removed."

"We think the puppet may be used to conceal something valuable," Nancy told Smitty. "Do you see anything in there?"

The police electrician pulled a small flashlight from

his pocket and trained it on the interior of the puppet. "Wait till you see what's here!" he cried out suddenly as he reached inside.

· 18 ·

The Hollow Laugh

THE three girls crowded forward to see what the police electrician was going to pull out from the back of the dancing puppet. The detectives kept a tight grip on Sam Longman in case he should try to get away again.

"A pearl necklace!" Bess squealed.

"Those look like genuine pearls," George commented.

"And obviously stolen too," Detective Foster spoke up.

By this time the police electrician had drawn out several more valuable necklaces—one of diamonds, another of sapphires, two of rubies and two more of pearls.

"These must be worth a fortune!" Bess exclaimed.

"They sure are," Detective Dougherty agreed. "We'll take it all down to headquarters. Well, Longman, what do you have to say now?"

Instead of replying, the prisoner suddenly went dead white and clutched at his heart. "I'm going to have an attack!" he said.

Instantly Dougherty led him into the bedroom, laid the man on the bed and felt his pulse.

"You're having no heart attack," he said acidly. "Your heart beats fast because you're scared, but that won't keep you out of jail. Come on!" He helped the man to his feet, and together the two detectives started for the door with him.

Dougherty turned to Nancy and her friends. "Would you girls mind staying here until we return?" he requested. "If any callers come, try to keep them here. We'll get this fellow booked as soon as possible and be right back."

The girls agreed to remain. While awaiting the detectives' return, Nancy examined the puppet herself. "My, what a maze of wires there are in here!"

Bess and George peered inside the back of the figure. "Whoever made this was an inventive genius," George remarked.

"Let's try to make the puppet dance by holding her up," Bess suggested with a giggle.

The three girls stood the puppet on its feet and manipulated its limbs and head from the various gadgets inside. Nancy and her friends were still playing with the puppet when Dougherty and Foster returned. The two detectives laughed heartily.

"I guess girls never get tired of playing with dolls," Dougherty said with a grin.

Nancy's eyes danced. "Especially when there's a mystery connected with one. I was just thinking— Longman never explained how he happened to be in possession of the dancing puppet."

"We tried to make him," Foster told her. "On the way to headquarters we asked him to explain the mystery of this puppet, but he kept insisting he knew nothing about any mystery. He said a friend of his had found the puppet in a junk shop. Being an electrician,

Longman had been intrigued enough to try making it work by putting in wires and batteries. He still insists he doesn't know how the stolen jewellery got inside."

"Do you think he's telling the truth?" Nancy asked the detectives.

The two men shrugged, and Detective Foster answered, "Even the mystery of the stolen jewellery is far from solved." He smiled. "The police certainly want to thank you girls for all your help. If you find out anything more, let us know!"

The three young sleuths laughed and promised to do this. Then they drove back towards the Van Pelt estate. Bess had seen a morning newspaper lying on a table in Longman's apartment and had helped herself to it. Now she began to read.

In the meantime, George and Nancy continued to discuss the mystery of the dancing puppet. "Do you think," George asked, "that there may be other members of a gang stealing jewellery and using the puppet as a hiding place until it's safe to sell the pieces?"

"That's a possibility, George," Nancy agreed. "If so—I'm wondering if we'll be bothered any more out at the mansion."

"How could we, with the puppet in the hands of the police?" George countered.

"There could be more puppets," Nancy replied. "We already know of two others."

George's reply was interrupted by Bess. "Listen to this!" she cried out, reading from an inside page of the newspaper. " 'Unknown Amateur Steals Show.' And underneath it says, 'Nancy Drew Makes Big Hit in First Performance.' "

"Oh, no!" Nancy exclaimed, blushing. "Why, that makes it look as if I were better than Tammi, and that's ridiculous."

"You *were* better than Tammi," Bess said staunchly.

"Just as good, anyway," conceded George. She suddenly laughed loudly. "If Tammi Whitlock sees this, she'll be back on stage tonight even if she sounds like a frog!"

Nancy was silent during the rest of the drive. She did not care for Tammi, yet she did not wish to make an enemy of her. Vividly Nancy recalled Chuck Grant's saying that his sister was a firebrand when she became angry. Nancy thought, "Why, there's no telling what Tammi may do!"

Upon reaching the estate, she parked the car, then the three girls went into the kitchen. Mr Spencer stood inside, a copy of the same newspaper in his hand. He wore a broad smile. "I suppose you know what the paper said about your performance, Nancy."

"Yes," she said quietly. "I'm glad my performance was good, but I hope that Tammi gets back here in a hurry."

Mr Spencer looked directly at Nancy. "Listen to me," he said. "Even if Tammi returns, you are going to continue in the leading role. I've had enough of her temperamental fits—and there are certain scenes in the play which she refuses to do according to my direction. Fortunately, you are co-operative."

Nancy was nonplussed. But finally she said, "Mr Spencer, don't think I'm not appreciative of this honour, but I couldn't continue to have an important part in any play. I help my father, you know, and I shouldn't try to hold down two jobs."

"I realize that," the actor said. "I'll talk to your father. I'm sure he'll see things my way."

Mr Spencer was making it very difficult for Nancy. She loved to act, but far more than this, she loved working on mystery cases, either with her father or on her own.

The actor went on, "Nancy, you can't let me down! Our new play goes on in a week, and you know what a sad state it's in right now. *Please* learn the lines. I think you have a good influence on the cast, and they'll probably work better with you than they did with Tammi."

Bess and George knew that Nancy was in a tight spot. Bess had a sudden inspiration. "Mr Spencer," she said, "I think I may have the answer to your problem. Why don't you substitute a puppet show for a couple of weeks until the next play can be whipped into shape?"

"Puppet show?" Mr Spencer echoed. "You must be teasing—your mind's been on the mystery of the dancing puppet too long."

"Oh, no, I'm not fooling," said Bess. "There's a long article in the paper about a marvellous European puppeteer who is touring this country and putting on magnificent shows. Maybe you could get him to help you out."

Mr Spencer had not seen the item. After Bess pointed it out and he had read the article, Mr Spencer scratched his head.

"Bess," he said, "you may have a point." Suddenly he became very enthusiastic about the idea. "I think it would be good to give the cast a rest. Maybe I've been pushing them too hard and they've gone stale. I'll make some phone calls right away and try to locate this fellow."

After he had left the kitchen, Nancy hugged Bess. "You're a lifesaver, dear," she said. "Let's keep our fingers crossed and hope that Mr Spencer will be able to engage that puppeteer!"

When Hamilton Spencer returned from the telephone, there was a broad smile on his face. "I've reserved the services of the puppeteer!" he announced. "The Floodlighters can vote on this tonight."

"Swell!" said George.

With this matter settled, Nancy now told Mr Spencer about finding the dancing puppet.

"And her back was filled with necklaces!" George announced.

The actor listened spellbound as the girls related the entire story. But he was as puzzled as they to know why Longman, and probably his pal Terrill, had made the puppet dance on the Van Pelt lawn. "What are we going to do now?" he asked. "Forget the whole thing and assume that the mystery is ended, even though it hasn't been entirely solved?"

Bess spoke up immediately. "Mr Spencer, if you want us to leave, I'm sure Nancy——"

"Oh, no!" the man answered quickly. "I didn't mean to imply that I wanted you to go away. Please don't do that!"

Mr Spencer became so embarrassed that Nancy felt sorry for him. She smiled sweetly. "I'd like to stay," she said. "It bothers me to leave a mystery unsolved. I'd like to do a little more investigating around this place to see if I can pick up another clue. Who knows, maybe the witch and the Pierrot have stolen valuables hidden in them!"

"Before we do another speck of sleuthing," Bess spoke up, "we're going to have lunch. I'm starved."

George began to laugh. "It would be good for you to go without it. How else can you lose those twenty pounds you've been talking about?"

Bess made a face at her cousin, then marched straight for the refrigerator. The first thing she pulled out of it was a large jar of mayonnaise.

"Uh-uh," said George, grabbing the jar from her cousin. "Your rations will be one piece of lettuce, one tomato, and one thin slice of roast beef."

"I *have* lost five pounds," Bess contended. "Let's not go overboard on this!" Then she sighed. "Oh, I suppose you're right." Mr Spencer had left the kitchen, so Bess added, "I still want to get a better part in the play than just the maid. She only has a few lines."

As soon as the girls had eaten and washed the dishes, Bess and George asked Nancy what she had in mind.

"Another trip to the attic," said Nancy. "I want to look at Pierrot again. He may be more valuable than we think."

George grinned. "You mean the clown may be full of diamonds? I always thought everything about a clown was make-believe. It's more likely he'd be wearing costume jewellery!"

The other girls laughed, and the three started for the attic in a merry but excited mood. Were they going to find something else connected with the mystery?

Once more, Bess stood guard at the top of the stairs.

George followed Nancy to the secret door and watched as her friend opened it. A cry of amazement burst from her lips.

Pierrot was gone!

As the girls stood staring in dismay at the empty cupboard, they heard an evil-sounding, hollow laugh!

A Puppeteer's Secret

"WH-WHAT's that?" Bess screamed in fright.

Nancy and George stood frozen to the spot. The hollow laugh was not repeated.

Nancy, sure the laugh had come from behind the back of the secret cupboard, began to look around for another opening. But though she scrutinized the wooden wall for several minutes, the young detective could not locate any hidden springs or latches. The cupboard walls seemed perfectly solid.

"I wonder what's on the other side of this," Nancy said, frowning.

She stepped from the cupboard and looked questioningly at her chums. Bess had come to the side of George, whose grim look and stance indicated she was poised to greet the mysterious laugher, should he appear.

"Maybe," Nancy said, "there's a roof behind this cupboard, and someone's standing there."

She ran to one of the small attic windows. After some difficulty she managed to open it and look outside. There was no roof beyond the cupboard, but Nancy saw that the cupboard itself formed the top of an extension of the main house.

"See anybody?" George asked.

"No."

As Nancy returned to her friends, Bess said in a tremulous whisper, "I'm beginning to think this place *is* haunted!"

Nancy laughed. "I'll think so too, until the mystery is solved and I know just who has been doing queer things around here. Personally, I believe Terrill and Longman are guilty."

"But they're both in jail!" Bess reminded her. "So they couldn't have given the hollow laugh."

Nancy had to admit her friend was right, but said, "They could have confederates."

The girls waited for several more minutes. There was no further disturbance and Nancy suggested that they start looking through the books stored in the attic. "We may find a clue tucked in one of them to help us solve the mystery."

Since there were three large boxes of them, the girls divided the work. For the next half hour there was silence in the attic as book after book was carefully examined, page by page. No papers, no letters, and no reading matter which was of any help to them came to light.

"This is a week's work," Bess said finally, giving a great sigh. "Let's take a rest and come back to the job later."

"Yes, let's," George agreed.

At that moment Nancy was deep in a small volume she had come across. It was the diary of a Ralph Van Pelt, written nearly fifty years before.

"I think I may have found something!" she told her friends excitedly. "Listen!"

She explained that Ralph Van Pelt had been an inventor, who had come to the United States from Holland. He had never married but had lived with a brother on the estate, which was then a farm. Every year, as Christmas gifts, he carved toys for his grandnieces and grandnephews.

"And guess what!" Nancy went on. "The children loved puppets, so their uncle used to make sets of them and put on little shows."

Bess and George, intrigued by the story, had come forward and seated themselves on the trunk to listen. Nancy now began to read the diary word for word. They learned from the well-written account that Ralph Van Pelt had become so interested in making puppets that he decided to try contriving life-size ones with mechanical devices inside to make them move. One section of the diary read:

" 'Today I had my first show out of doors. Relatives and friends were here for a Fourth of July picnic. Two of my marionettes performed very well. One danced and the other, a witch, frightened the children out of their wits!' "

"The puppets we found!" George exclaimed.

"What a clever man he must have been!" Bess commented. "I wonder how many puppets he made in all?"

Nancy read on. Presently she came to a passage which said that the grandnieces and grandnephews had nearly ruined one of the puppets playing with it. " 'So I decided to hide the marionettes,' " Van Pelt had written. " 'I built a secret cupboard in the attic and placed my four puppets inside for safety.' "

"Four!" George repeated. "Then one is still missing!"

"Probably Terril and Longman have it some place," said Bess.

Nancy did not agree. "I'm positive that the reason they were displaying the dancing puppet here was to scare people away from this mansion. Those men, or pals of theirs, could then have more freedom to search this place for the fourth puppet. But why did they want it so badly? Well, let me read some more."

There were several pages in the diary which had no bearing on the present mystery. Then suddenly Nancy came across an exciting item. It read:

" 'I took one of my puppets from the secret cupboard today. Inside the puppet I deposited a valuable secret. It would not help anyone today, but I assume the puppet will not be found for some years to come. When it is, the secret will make the finder wealthy. I hereby decree that whoever does find the puppet shall become the true owner of its secret.' "

Nancy paused, and the three girls looked at one another in complete amazement. What was the secret? And where was the puppet? Had it been stolen, or was it still in its hiding place?

"I certainly hope we can find that puppet!" George muttered.

Nancy said pieces of the puzzle were beginning to fall into place now. "I believe someone found this diary and read it not too long ago," she said. "I'm sure he was still hunting for the fourth puppet up to the time of the dancer's last appearance."

"Then it could still be here!" George exclaimed.

Nancy nodded. "On the other hand, it may have

been found years ago by someone who already has made use of the secret." Nancy's eyes roamed the attic, trying to imagine a hiding place for it.

Suddenly Bess spoke up. "Don't you think we'd better give up our attic sleuthing for now? Someone in this house may get suspicious and come up here. After all, Cally old boy hasn't been eliminated as a suspect in this case."

Before Nancy had a chance to reply, she heard Mr Spencer calling her from the first floor. She hurried downstairs, followed by Bess and George.

"I'd like you to go over some of the lines in the show," he told Nancy. "You did very well last night, and I want everything to run just as smoothly this evening. We'll have an early supper and go over to the theatre for a rehearsal."

As they were finishing dessert, Mr Spencer was called to the telephone. Nancy waited and waited for him to finish. Since the conversation went on and on, she decided to go over to the theatre herself and practise some of her lines.

"Bess, will you please tell Mr Spencer where I am?" she asked, as she opened the kitchen door to leave.

"Will do," Bess promised. "See you later. Good luck!"

Nancy quickly crossed the yard and went in the side entrance of the theatre, which was unlocked. She had not made a sound in her soft-soled shoes, so anyone inside would not have become aware of her presence.

Suddenly Nancy stopped dead in her tracks. Were her eyes deceiving her? The theatre was only dimly lighted, but she was sure her imagination was not playing tricks on her.

A life-size puppet was dancing jerkily across the stage!

"That must be the missing puppet!" Nancy told herself. "But someone has put a modern dress on it!"

Though moving jerkily, this figure was far more graceful than the dancing puppet Nancy had seen performing on the lawn.

Reaching the far side of the stage, the figure disappeared into the wings. At once Nancy ran after it. But before she herself had reached the opposite wing of the stage, the puppet suddenly returned. To Nancy's amazement, it came at her and began to attack her wildly with its arms and legs!

Warding off the blows, Nancy reached out to hold the puppet back. At this point she received a distinct shock. The puppet's body was warm! This was not a wood-and-plaster figure. It was a human being, wearing a mask!

Now Nancy fought with the attacker, and managed to pull off the mask.

"Tammi!" Nancy cried out, astounded.

"Yes, I'm Tammi," the other girl flung back in a hoarse whisper. "I'll teach you to steal my part in the show!"

In a frenzied rage the jealous girl grabbed Nancy and began to hit her with her fists!

· 20 ·

An Amazing Revelation

"Do you know what I'm going to do?" Tammi Whitlock panted as she tried to strike Nancy in the face. "I'm going to fix you so your acting career——"

Before she had a chance to finish her sentence, Mr Spencer came dashing on to the stage. His face was livid as he cried out, "What's the meaning of this? Tammi Whitlock, stop that!"

Without waiting for her to obey, he yanked the actress away from Nancy.

"While I've been home with laryngitis, you've been getting away with something out here, haven't you, Hamilton Spencer?" Tammi screamed hoarsely. "You didn't ask *me* about putting on a puppet show! Emmet Calhoun told me about it on the phone. I had other plans for the Footlighters—much better plans."

Nancy, weak from the battle with Tammi, sat down on a couch. She managed to describe to Mr Spencer her sudden encounter with Tammi as a dancing puppet.

"Yes, I was practising," Tammi went on, "so I could ruin that next show. I was going to come on as a puppet and spoil everything. I'll still do it!" she croaked.

Mr Spencer, now that he had recovered from his

astonishment, glared at the girl. "You'll do nothing of the sort," he said. "Furthermore, I shall see to it that you are asked to resign from the Footlighters!"

"You wouldn't dare!" Tammi could barely whisper now.

At this moment Emmet Calhoun rushed out on the stage to see what the commotion was. At once Tammi flew at him, her eyes blazing, and said in a fierce whisper, "You're the one who started everything going wrong. If you'd kept away from me, my brother wouldn't be in such a jam, you poetry-spouting old fossil!"

This remark angered Calhoun so much that he turned white. "You would do better to study Shakespeare," he retorted stiffly, "instead of running around with night-club performers. There was a time when I thought a great deal of you. But now I see I was wrong."

"That's enough!" said Tammi as loudly and vehemently as her laryngitis would permit. "You'd better keep still."

But Emmet Calhoun, now that he had started, had no intention of keeping quiet. Turning to Nancy, he said, "I have eavesdropped on you and your friends ever since you came here, because I was interested to find out whether you could locate the lost puppet."

Nancy looked at the actor in astonishment. "*You* knew about the diary?" she asked.

"I was idly browsing around the attic one day and found the diary in the trunk where you saw it," Calhoun replied. "When I first met Tammi and took a liking to her, I realized the great difference in our ages and thought I would need to offer her something really

valuable in order to win her. So, foolishly, I told
Tammi what I had read in the diary.

"I expected she would keep the information to herself, and that together we would hunt for the lost
puppet. Tammi just made fun of the idea, so I gave it
up. But she had a little scheme of her own. Tammi told
me you heard that Chuck Grant is her brother. She
had told him the story of the valuable hidden secret
and he in turn sold the information to two men named
Terrill and Longman."

Nancy was amazed to learn of Tammi's involvement.
She looked at the actress and said, "So you're tied in
with the mystery of the dancing puppet!"

"I never had anything to do with the puppets,"
Tammi maintained stoutly, "except that I did telephone to you once and say I was the dancing puppet. I
overheard Mr Spencer's plan to see your father,
Nancy, so I knew about you Drews. I mentioned it to
Chuck, and he told Longman, who'd heard of your
detecting. He happened to be around here the day you
arrived. It was Terrill and Longman who made all
the trouble here."

"Did you know," Nancy asked her, "that both men
are in jail?"

"N-no! Oh, it can't be true!" Tammi looked as if
she were about to faint.

Realizing this, Mr Spencer helped the actress to the
couch on stage. As the whole group sat down, he
urged Tammi to tell all she knew about the crooked
dealings of Terrill and Longman.

Tammi did not speak, so Nancy, now filling in the
gaps in the mystery and doing a bit of guesswork, told

what she knew of the story. She said the two men had found the cannon balls, probably in the attic, and had hidden them in the hay until they found a market for them.

"When I came here to try to find out about the dancing puppet," Nancy went on, "one of these men followed me upstairs with the doll's trunk containing a cannon ball. He hurled the trunk at me, hoping everyone would think it was an accident."

Tammi began to cry. She nodded in agreement. With hardly any voice left, the young actress said, "I'll tell you the rest of the story. It was Longman who did that. He later sold the cannon balls to a museum for a good price. He also persuaded me to make that witch phone call—and to spy on you one night. But I didn't realize why.

"My brother Chuck is not a bad guy—he's just always in need of money," Tammi went on. "Terrill and Longman had come to the Green Acres Restaurant several times and became acquainted with Chuck. Once when he needed some quick cash, they obliged him.

"After that, he seemed to be in their clutches. Finally they asked him to help them with a necklace-lifting racket. For a long time I didn't realize what was going on. I'd go to the various other places where Chuck sang. During his breaks, he'd always talk about the expensive jewellery the women were wearing and asked me to point out someone with a real diamond necklace, or one of pearls or rubies or other valuable stones.

"Then in a little while he would say we had to leave.

I would go out to the car and wait for him. In a few minutes Chuck would join me.

"After one of these singing engagements, he had slung his jacket over into the back seat of the car, and I saw a diamond necklace fall out of the pocket. When I demanded an explanation, he was forced to confess he was working with Terrill and Longman. Chuck would help distract the patron while Terrill would cut the necklace from the patron's neck. Longman would gently lift it and quick as a wink drop it into Chuck's pocket. Then Chuck would leave.

"I begged my brother to get out of the racket, but he insisted he couldn't. The men had told him he was in it too deep and that they would soon have enough money so all three could quit the racket before the police caught up with them."

Tammi paused. Then she faced Nancy. "Believe it or not, I'm glad the whole thing is over. I've done nothing but worry for weeks. It has made me cranky and hard to live with. I hope all of you will forgive me. I suppose I'll be punished for my part in this thing. But as soon as I'm free again, I'm going to be strictly honest and go back to the legitimate stage."

The others stared at her.

"You aren't an amateur?" Calhoun cried out.

Tammi shook her head. "In California I had parts in repertory theatre. When I came East my parents requested that I pretend to be an amateur. They didn't want me to be on the legitimate stage." Tammi buried her face in her hands. "Don't feel sorry for me. I deserve this. I just feel terribly sorry for my mother and father and aunt. They're going to be crushed when the news comes out."

She rose from the couch. With Mr Spencer and Emmet Calhoun, walking on each side of her, she left the theatre and went over to the mansion. Nancy learned later that the police had been notified to pick up Tammi and Chuck.

Presently the two actors returned to the theatre. "We must get backstage," said Mr Spencer. "Nancy, we've used up all our rehearsal time, but to very good advantage."

Nancy, still dazed by Tammi's confession, nodded. Then she said to Mr Spencer, "Have the prisoners said where they found the puppets?"

"In the attic," the actor answered. "The witch and the dancing girl were in a trunk, so evidently someone removed them from the cupboard a long time ago."

Mr Spencer said Chief McGinnis had also told him that Terril and Longman finally had talked freely about the puppets. The two prisoners had said that they used the dancer to scare residents away from the Van Pelt estate, so they could make a more thorough search. Moreover, they had wanted to test the puppets mechanically, so they could sell or rent them for a fancy price.

"Nancy, when you discovered Pierrot, Longman was hiding in the attic. Later he took the puppet."

"That means the fourth puppet—the special one—is still missing!" said Nancy. "After the show tonight, let's hunt for it! I still want to know the valuable secret it contains!"

That evening's show was another overwhelming success. To make matters more interesting, Bess had been asked to play the part of a minor character. The girl who was to have taken the role had suddenly become ill. Bess, excited and happy and looking extremely pretty, played the part well. Lines she could not remember she improvised, and her performance brought a good round of applause from the audience.

As soon as the show was over, the Footlighters were called together by the Spencers to vote on the idea of a puppet show. There was unanimous acceptance of the plan. Then the actors returned to the mansion and removed costumes and make-up. Congratulations and good-nights were said.

As soon as everyone had left, Nancy and the others living in the house hurried to the attic.

"I have a hunch that the fourth puppet is hidden somewhere near the secret cupboard," Nancy said.

One by one, trunks and boxes were moved. With a flashlight the girl detective examined the floor carefully. Finally she decided on a spot and asked the men to help her pry up the floor boards.

George and Bess each held a flashlight. Margo looked on intently. Suddenly one of the wider boards came free. Below lay a handsome male dancer puppet in Spanish costume!

"We've found it!" Bess exclaimed gleefully. She whirled round, causing her light to shine in another direction.

"Bring that light back here!" Mr Spencer called excitedly.

He and Emmet Calhoun, with Nancy and Margo helping, pulled up another floor board. The hidden puppet was freed.

"He looks almost real!" George remarked.

Nancy was already lifting his velvet bolero and white silk blouse to look at his back. In it was a door with a tiny knob. Quickly she turned it and opened the little door.

"Papers!" she cried.

Nancy pulled them out and with a quick reading of the first page discovered that here were the directions and working drawings for a clever invention.

Mr Spencer was extremely interested. "I studied engineering before I switched to acting," he said. "These drawings are of a device that we now call 'fuel cells'—machines for continuously producing electricity from chemical fuels. The Van Pelt type was to be used on melted aluminium. Of course, fifty years ago that element cost too much to make this invention feasible. But today, with aluminium inexpensive, it's a very worth-while idea."

"Oh, Nancy, you found it!" Bess cried proudly. "It's yours! You can sell it for a mint of money."

Nancy smiled and shook her head. "This discovery belongs to the Footlighters, and any money it may bring will go to them."

During the momentary silence following Nancy's announcement, the group in the attic heard a voice from downstairs calling, "Anybody home?"

Quickly Mr Spencer descended the stairs, with the others at his heels. When they reached the main hall, everyone burst into laughter. There stood Chief McGinnis, grinning sheepishly. Under one arm he was carrying the Pierrot puppet; under the other, the witch!

Behind him, just coming through the doorway was Detective Dougherty, lugging the dancing puppet. Chief McGinnis explained that the two missing puppets had been found in Terrill's apartment. Both had contained several pieces of valuable jewellery.

Just as the explanation was finished, the front doorbell rang. Mr Spencer opened the door.

"Good evening, Mr Trask," he said. "Come in." The actor introduced the caller as the owner of the puppet show which would be presented in the theatre a week from that night.

Mr Trask barely acknowledged the introduction. His eyes opening wide, he asked, "Where did these marvellous marionettes come from? If they're for sale, I want to buy them. How much are you asking for them?"

Despite the fact that the caller was serious, the whole situation seemed so comical that everyone smiled. Emmet Calhoun threw back his head and gave a long, hollow laugh.

Nancy looked at him in amazement. "You were the one who laughed behind the secret cupboard! How did you do it?"

Emmet Calhoun stopped laughing long enough to say, "Nancy Drew, I'm surprised you didn't discover the secret stairway which leads from the cupboard in my room to the back of that little attic cupboard. I'm a bit of a detective too, you see. I imagine that stairway opened into the attic years ago." Gaily he quoted the lines from *King John:*

     "'*The day shall not be up so soon as I,*
       To try the fair adventure of tomorrow.'"

"That fits me," thought Nancy. "I'm ready for a new mystery to solve, even if it's before dawn!" Fate was waiting for her to take on *The Clue of the Tapping Heels*.

The caller, Mr Trask, who had been looking on in astonishment, now repeated his offer to buy the puppets.

"More money for the Footlighters!" George exclaimed. "Nancy's not only an ace detective, but a money-maker and a top actress!"

Nancy waved aside the praise. "The club will vote, of course, on what to do with the puppets; but if you ask me," she added, her eyes twinkling, "we should keep the dancing puppet and her friends. They may come in handy sometime, when a live performance isn't ready to go on!"

Mr Spencer laughed heartily. "Detective Drew," he said, "you're absolutely right. Puppets saved us once, and these just might save us again!"

The Nancy Drew Mystery Stories

by Carolyn Keene

Have you read all the titles in this exciting mystery series? Look out for these new titles coming in 1989:

No. 43 **The Secret of Red Gate Farm**
No. 44 **The Secret of the Wooden Lady**
No. 45 **The Hidden Window Mystery**
No. 46 **The Clue of the Whistling Bagpipes**

ARMADA

HAVE YOU SEEN NANCY DREW LATELY?

Nancy Drew has become a girl of the 80s! There is hardly a girl from seven to seventeen who doesn't know her name.

Now you can continue to enjoy Nancy Drew in a new series, written for older readers – THE NANCY DREW FILES. Each book has more romance, fashion, mystery and adventure.

Join Nancy in all these fabulous adventures, available only in Armada:

No. 1 Secrets Can Kill ☐
No. 2 Deadly Intent ☐
No. 3 Murder on Ice ☐
No. 4 Smile and Say Murder ☐
No. 5 Hit-and-Run Holiday ☐
No. 6 White Water Terror ☐

All £1.95

To order direct from the publishers just tick the titles you want and send your name and address with a cheque/postal order for the price of the book plus postage to:

Collins Childrens Cash Sales
PO Box 11
Falmouth
Cornwall
TR10 9EP

Postage: 60p for the first book, 25p for the second book, plus 15p per copy thereafter, to a maximum of £1.90.

ARMADA

The Nancy Drew Files

by Carolyn Keene

Don't miss these new titles in the Nancy Drew Files, coming in Armada in 1989:

ARMADA